Be like Batty—read them all!

Shark and Bot

+ More *Shark and Bot* coming soon!

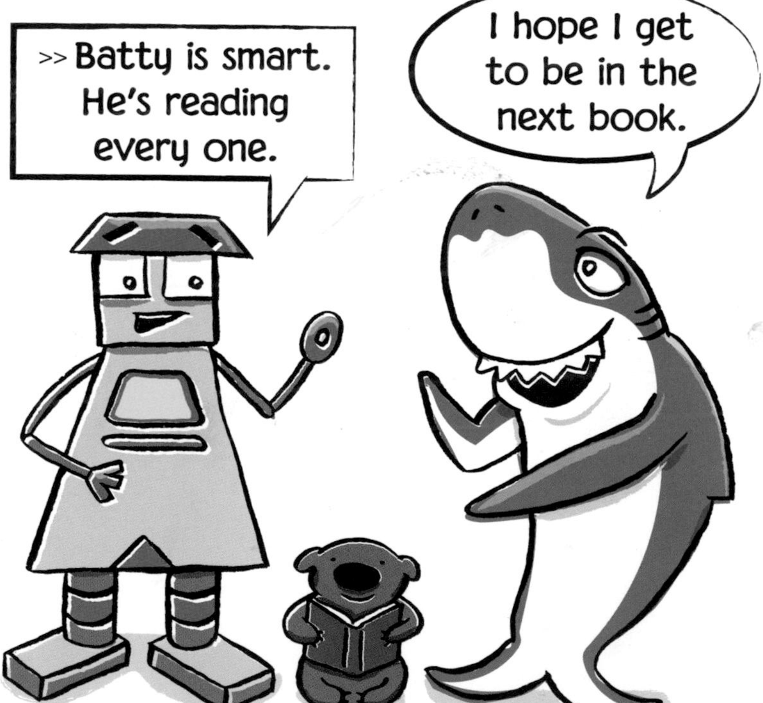

>> Batty is smart. He's reading every one.
I hope I get to be in the next book.

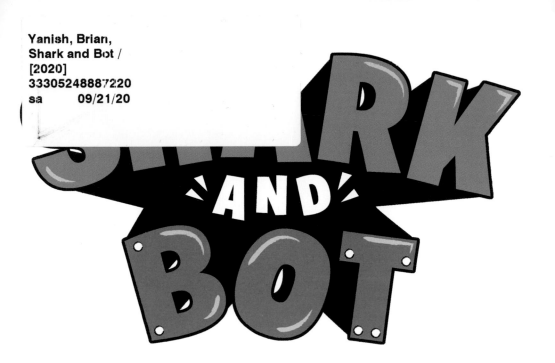

SHARK AND BOT

Brian Yanish

Random House 🏠 New York

All rights reserved. Published in the United States by Random House Children's Books,
a division of Penguin Random House LLC, New York.

Random House and the colophon are registered trademarks of Penguin Random House LLC.

Visit us on the Web! rhcbooks.com

Educators and librarians, for a variety of teaching tools, visit us at RHTeachersLibrarians.com

Library of Congress Cataloging-in-Publication Data
Names: Yanish, Brian, author.
Title: Shark and Bot / Brian Yanish.
Description: New York : Random House Children's Books, [2020] I Series:
Shark and Bot ; 1 I Audience: Ages 5–8. I Summary: An unlikely friendship forms
between a great white shark and a robot when they bond over a favorite book series,
then stand—and dance—together against playground bullies.
Identifiers: LCCN 2019056518 (print) I LCCN 2019056519 (ebook) I ISBN 978-0-593-17335-0
(hardcover) I ISBN 978-0-593-17336-7 (lib. bdg.) I ISBN 978-0-593-17337-4 (ebook)
Subjects: CYAC: Friendship—Fiction. I White shark—Fiction. I Sharks—Fiction.
Robots—Fiction. I Bullying—Fiction. I Humorous stories.
Classification: LCC PZ7.1.Y368 Sh 2020 (print) I LCC PZ7.1.Y368 (ebook) I DDC [E]—dc23

Book design by Jan Gerardi

MANUFACTURED IN CHINA

10 9 8 7 6 5 4 3 2 1

First Edition

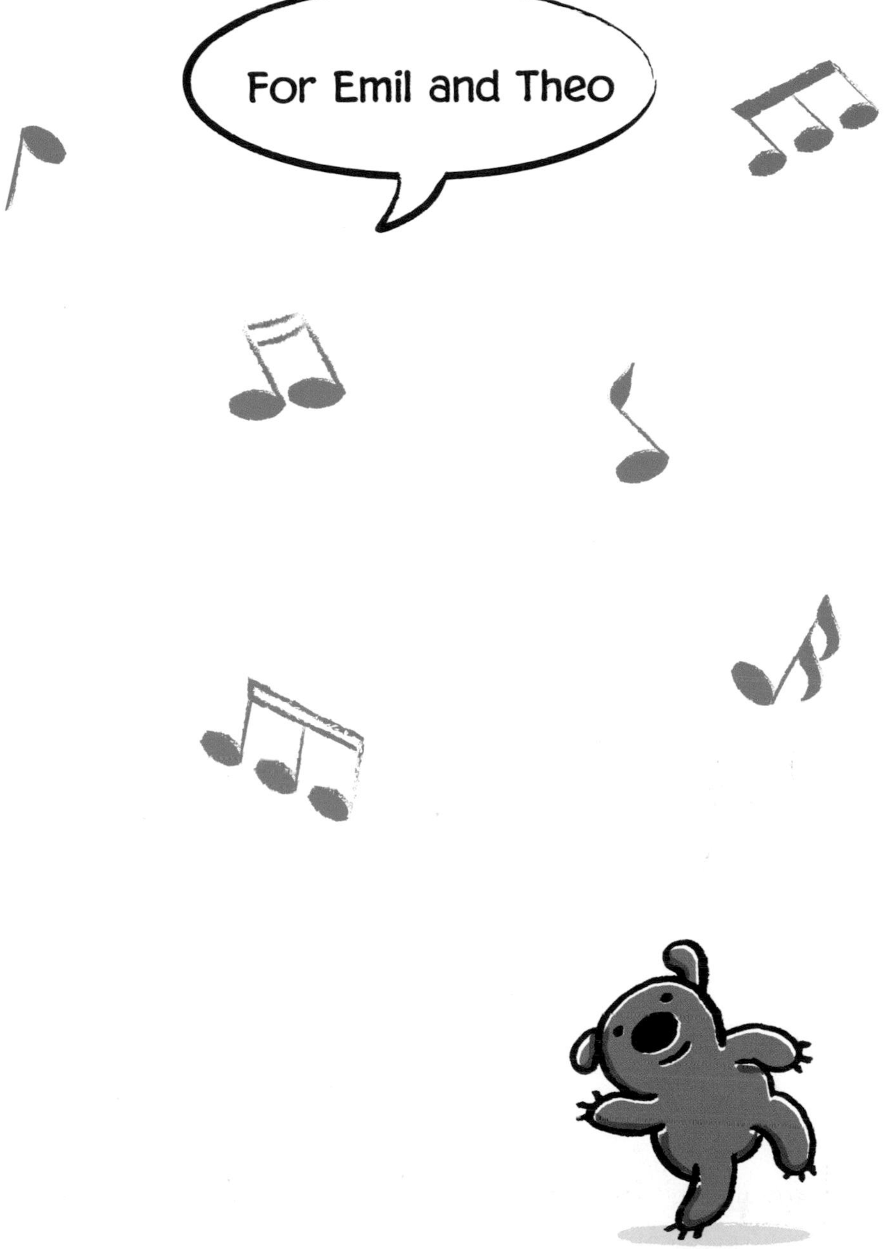
For Emil and Theo

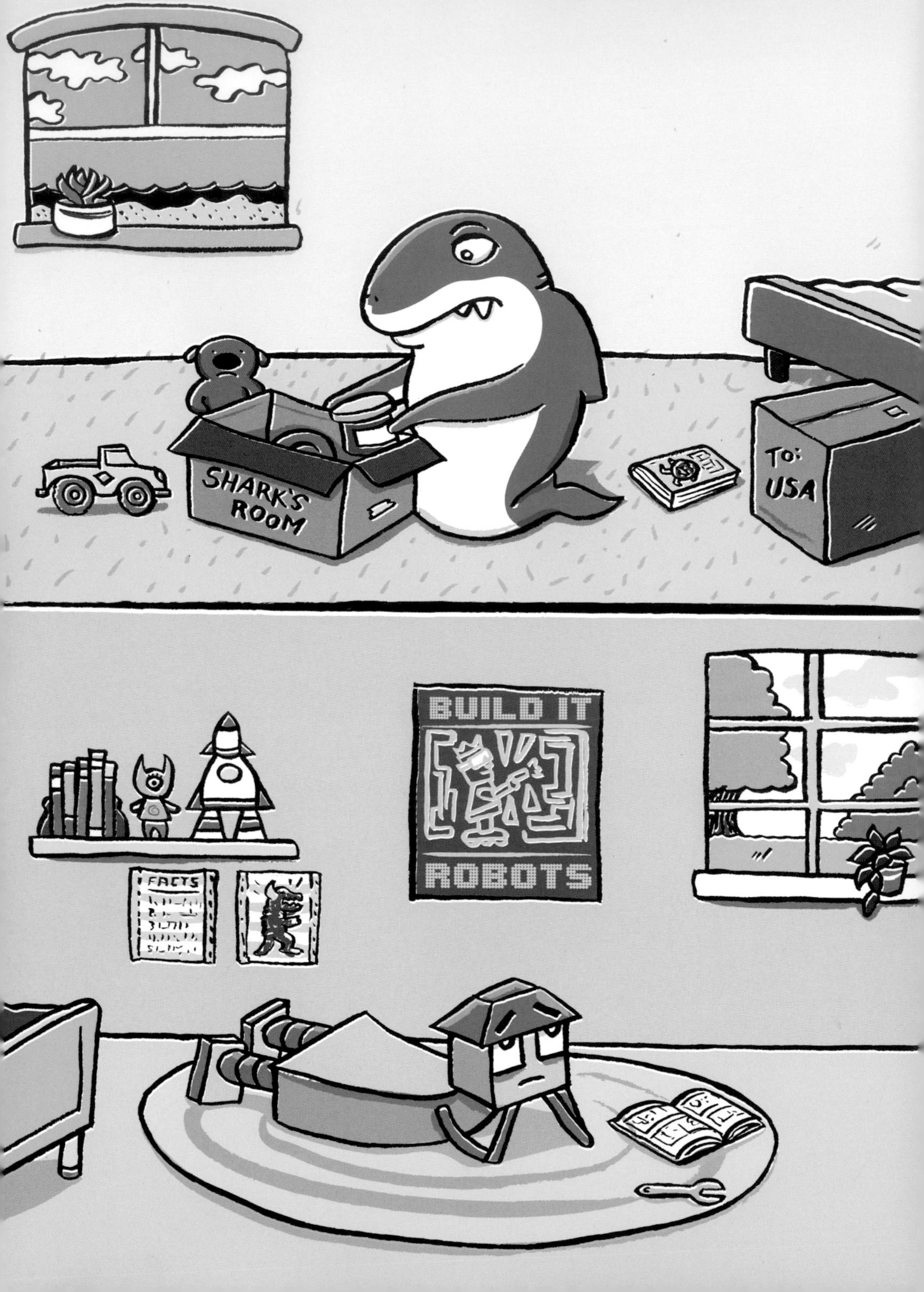

SHARK'S ROOM
TO: USA
BUILD IT
ROBOTS
FACTS

Contents

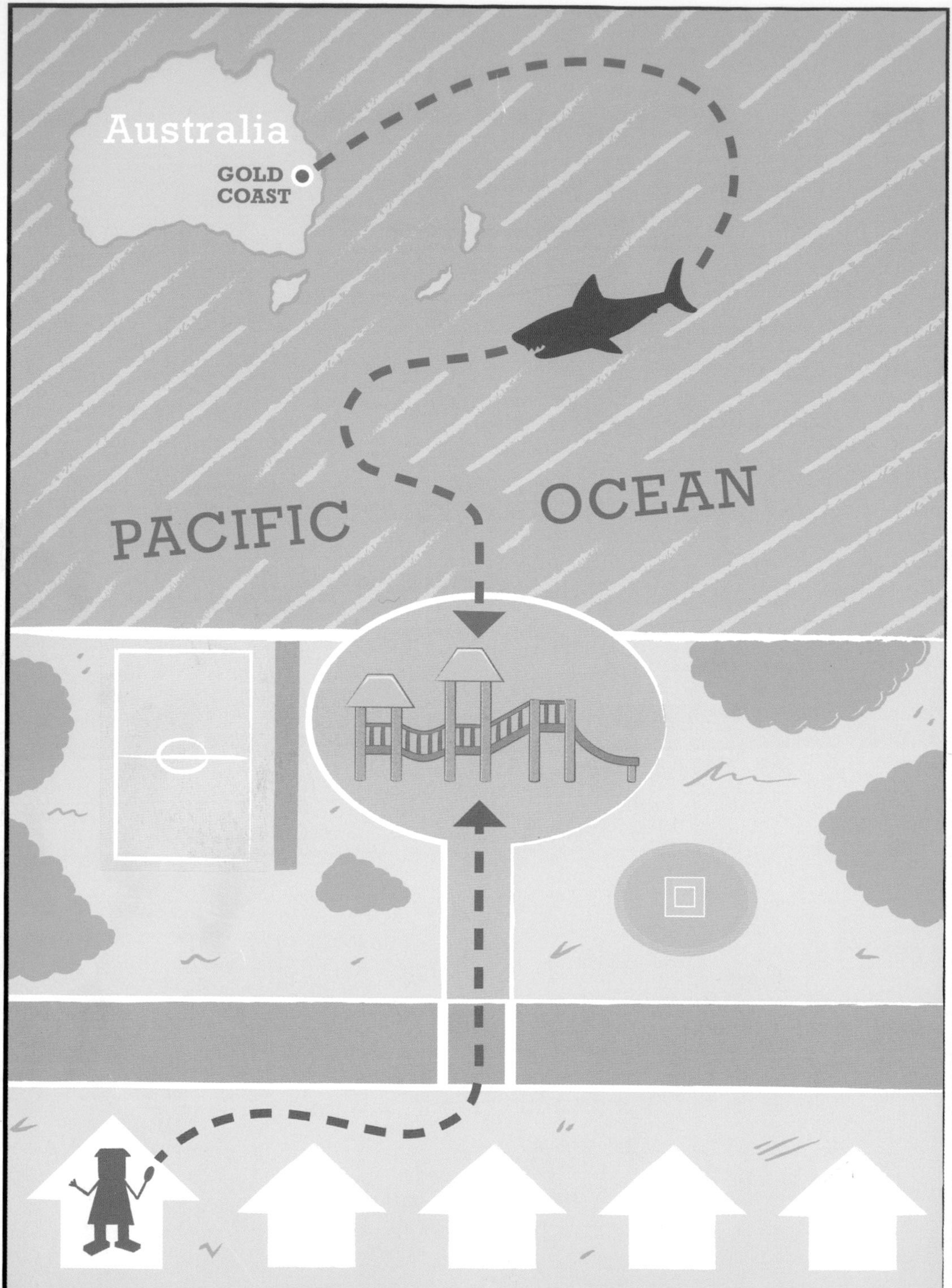
Australia
GOLD COAST
PACIFIC OCEAN

Chapter 1

First Contact

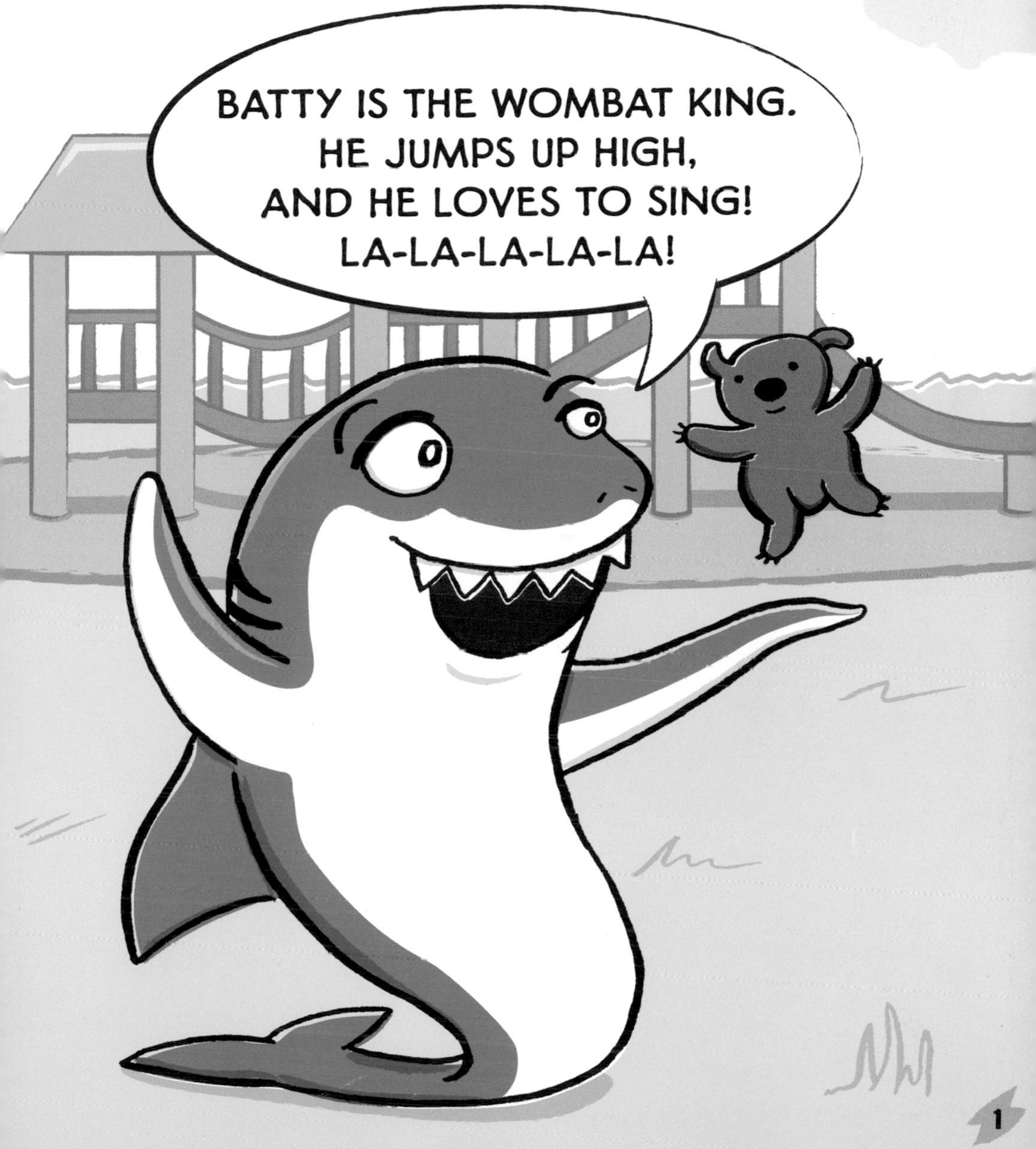
BATTY IS THE WOMBAT KING.
HE JUMPS UP HIGH,
AND HE LOVES TO SING!
LA-LA-LA-LA-LA!

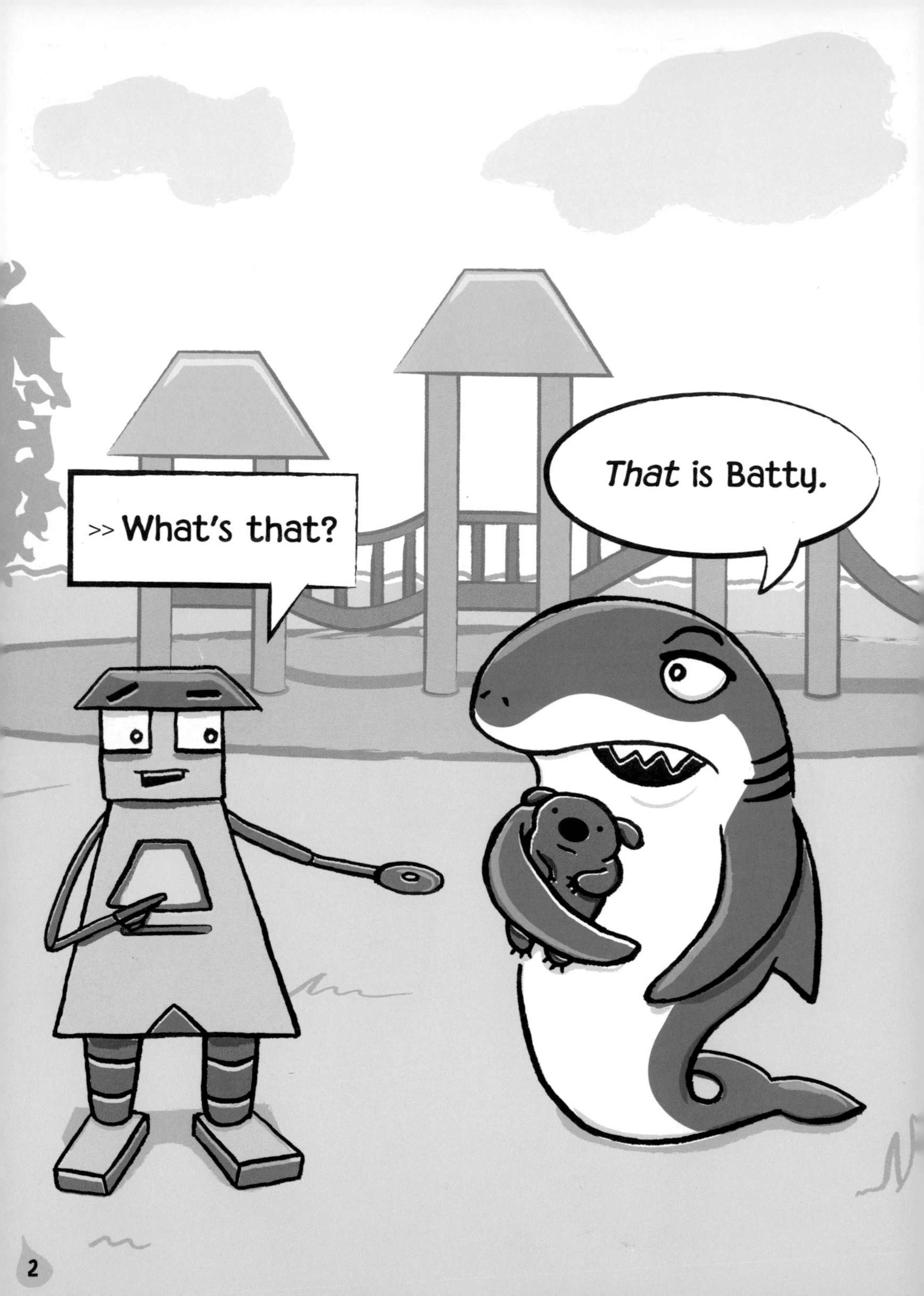
>> What's that?
That is Batty.

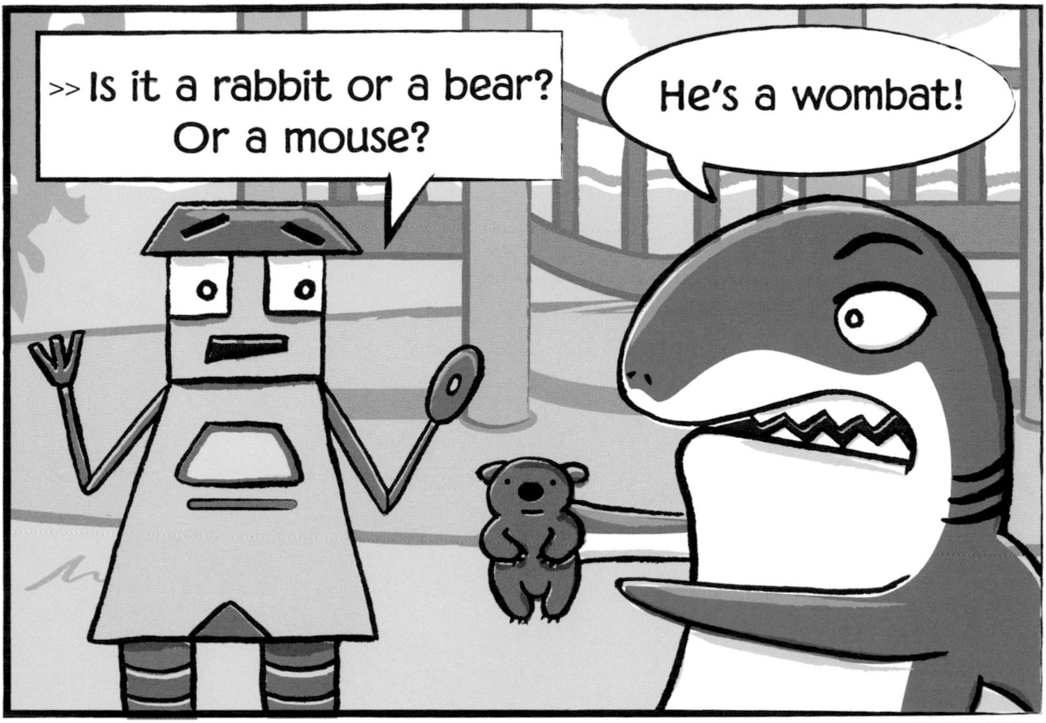
>> Is it a rabbit or a bear? Or a mouse?
He's a wombat!

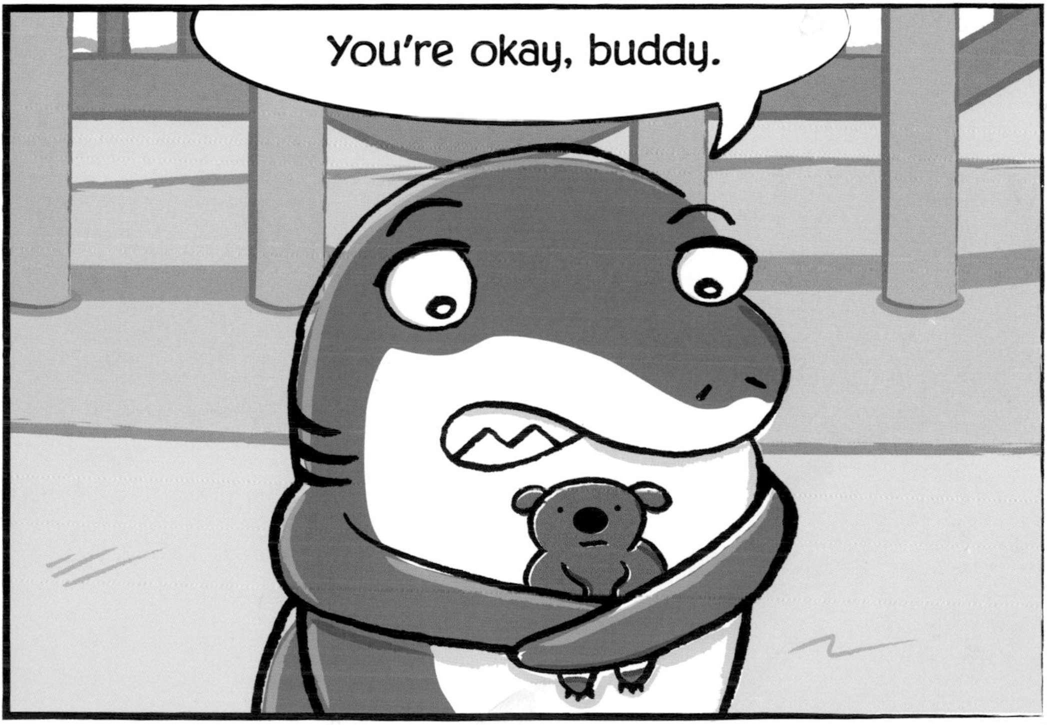
You're okay, buddy.

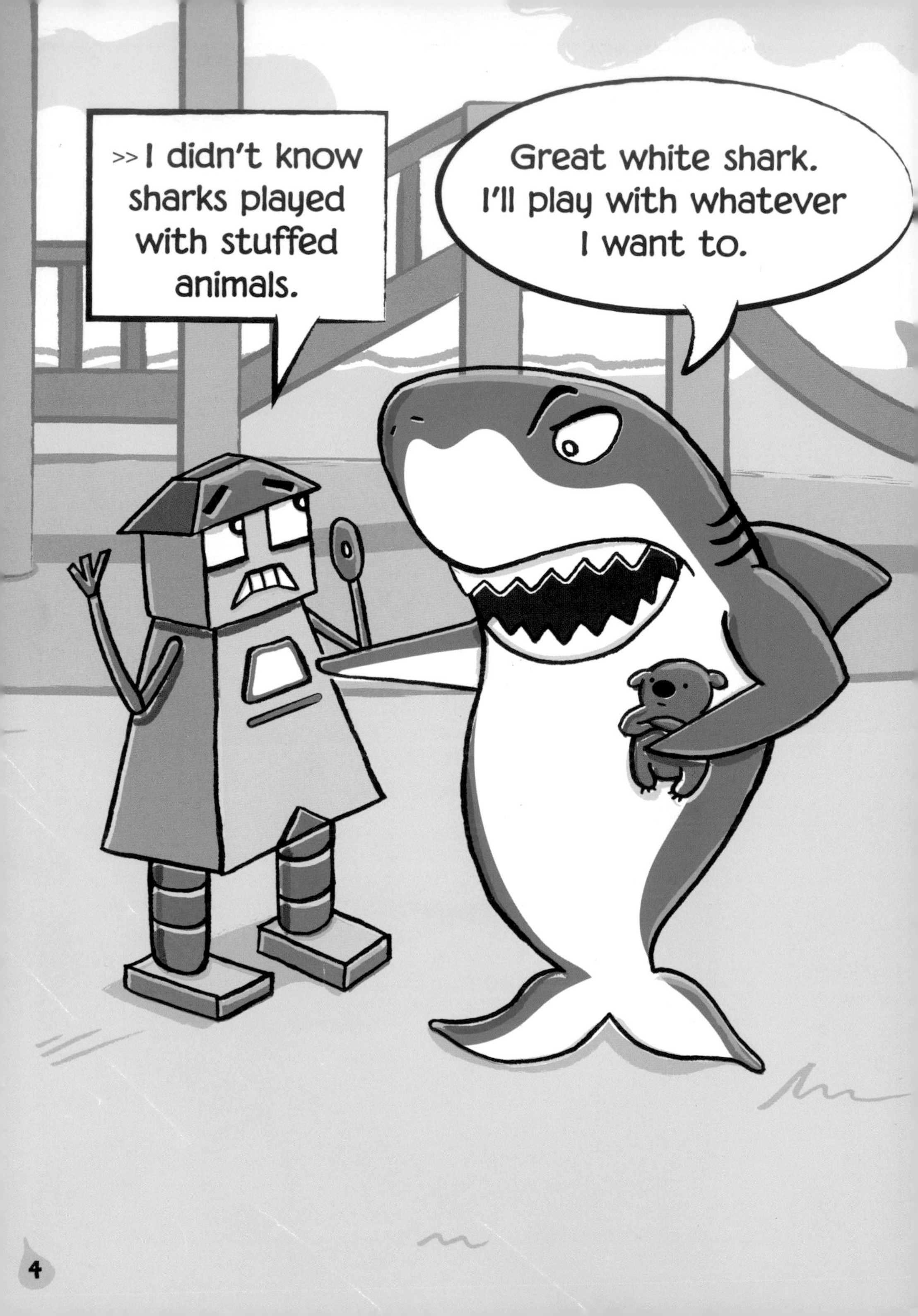
>> I didn't know sharks played with stuffed animals.
Great white shark. I'll play with whatever I want to.

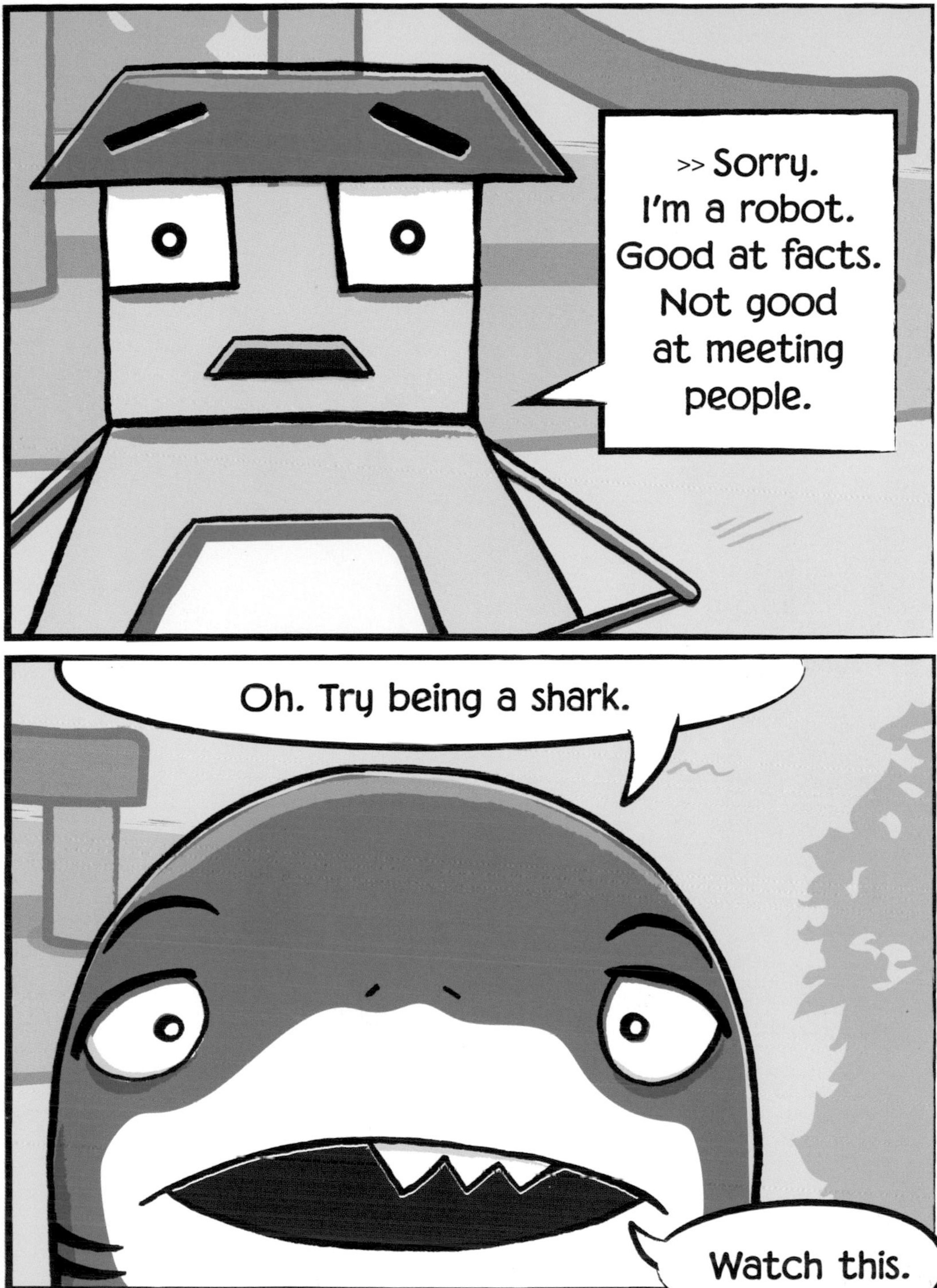

>> Sorry. I'm a robot. Good at facts. Not good at meeting people.
Oh. Try being a shark.
Watch this.

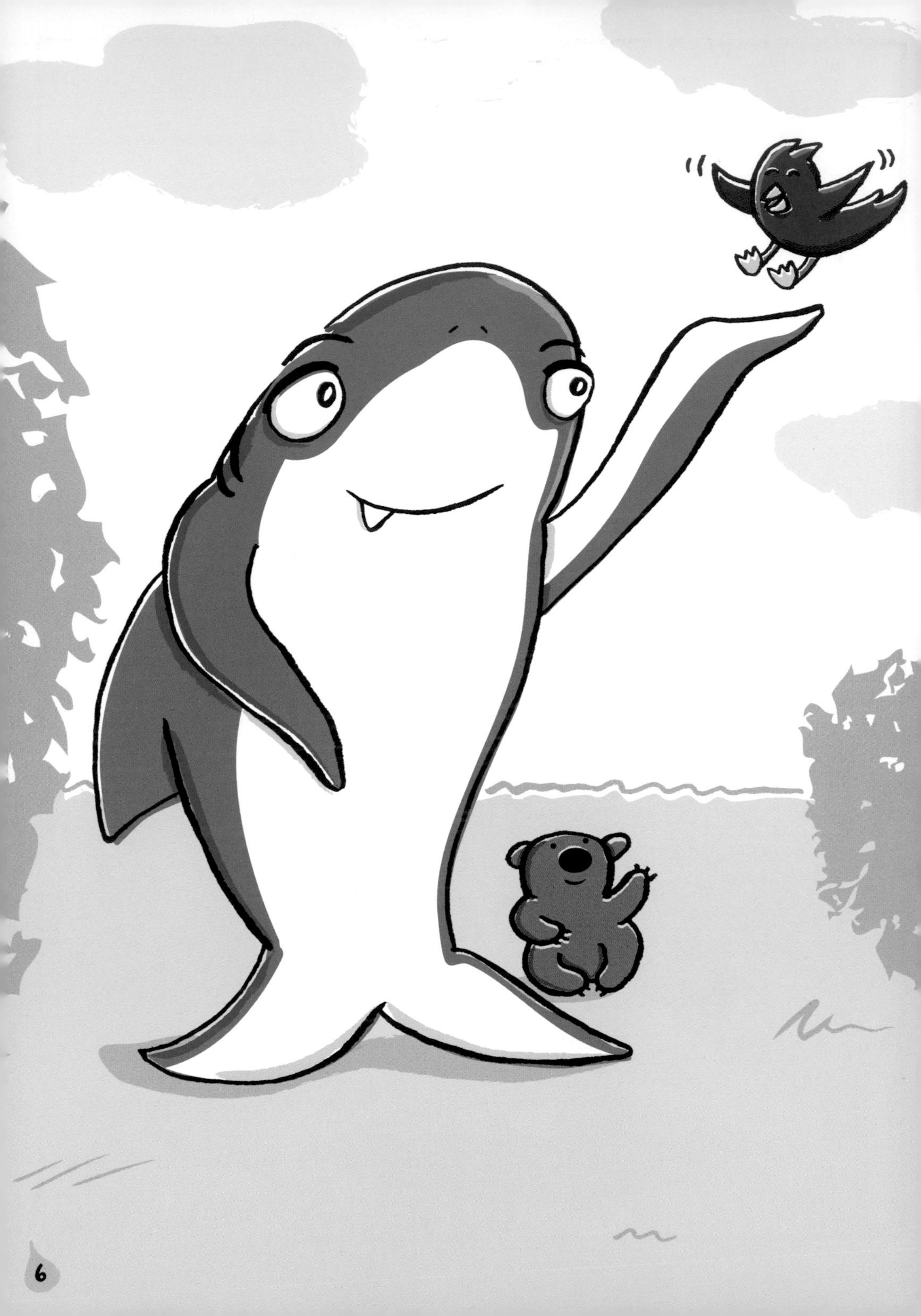

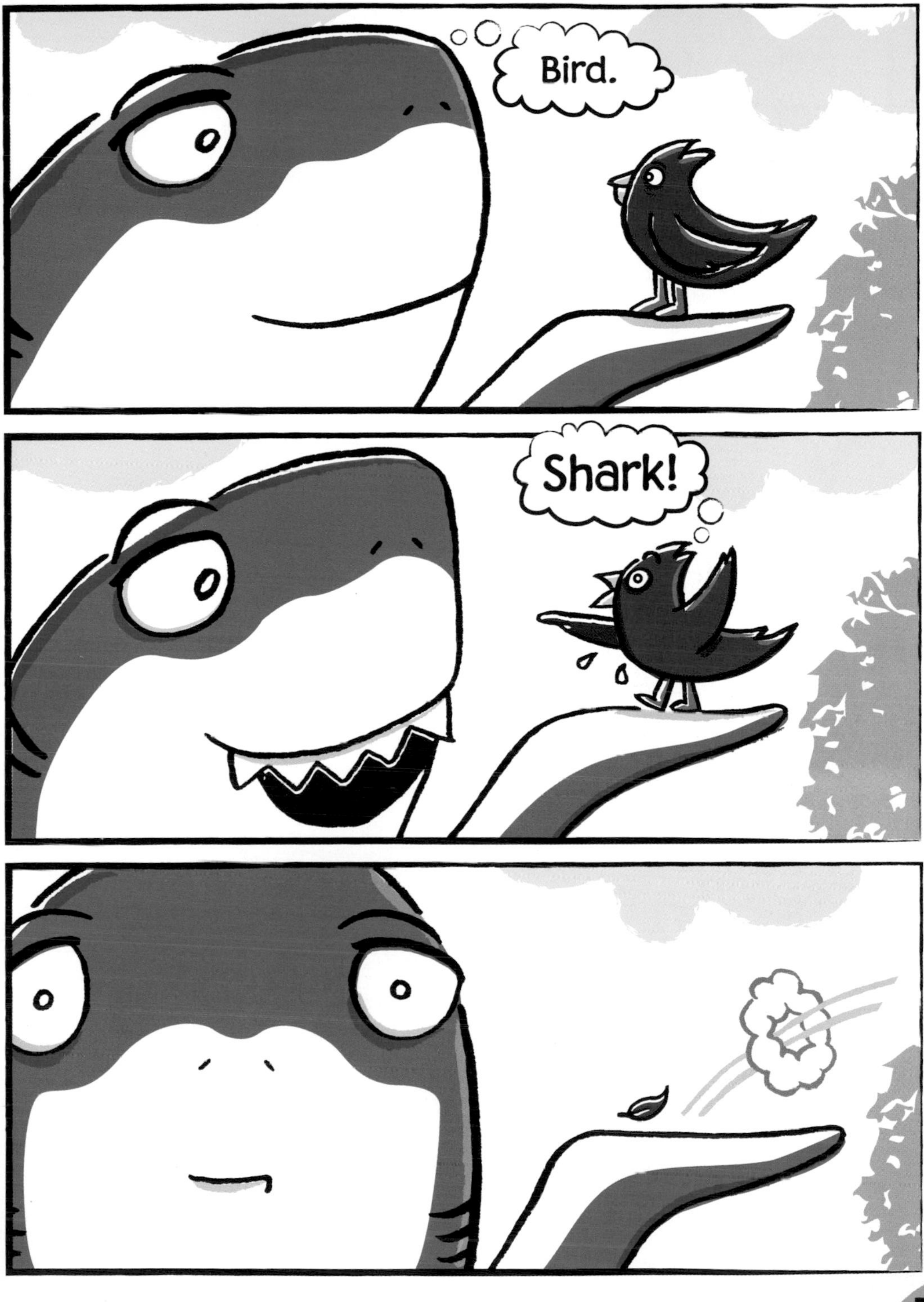
Bird.
Shark!

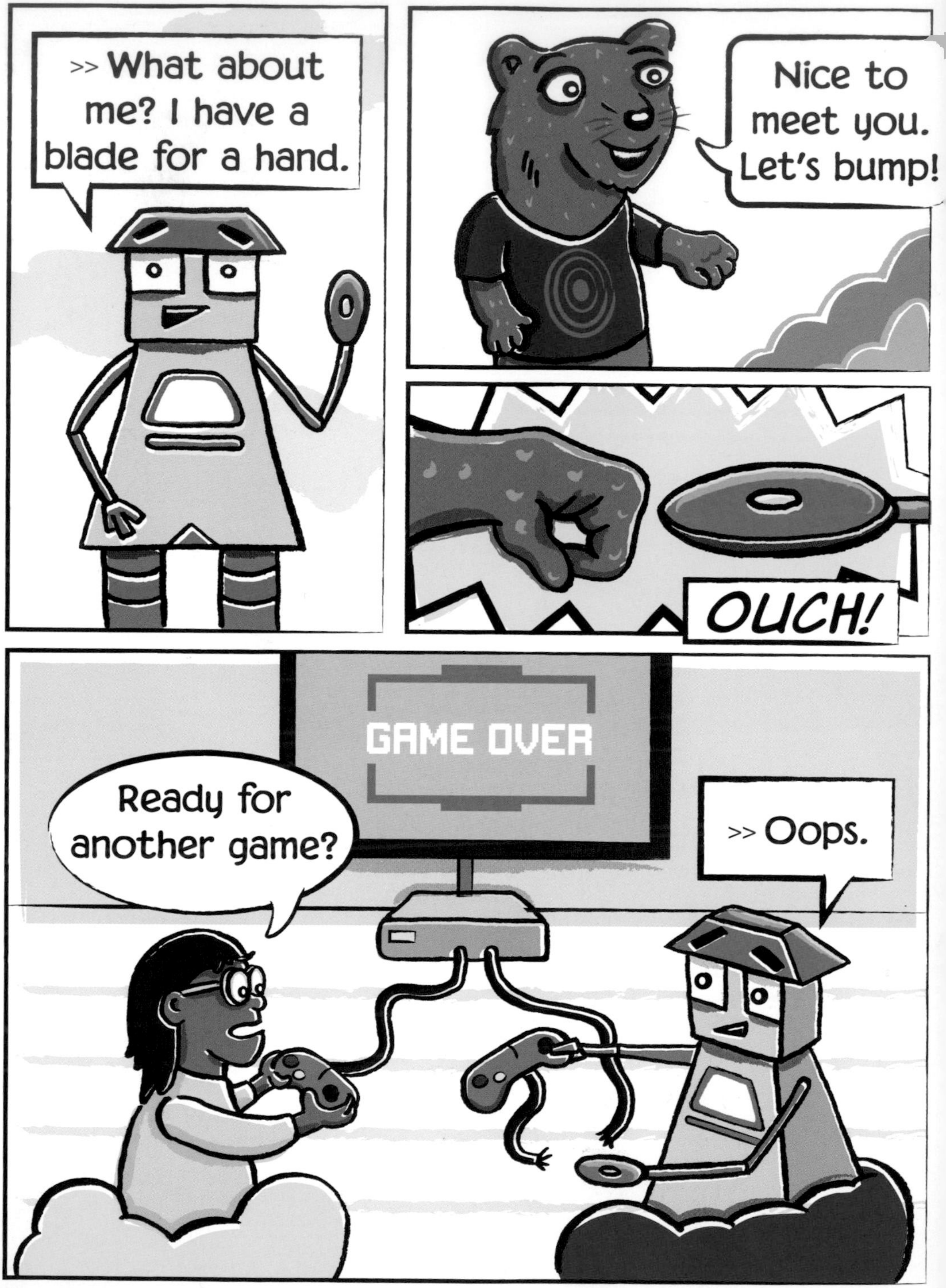
>> What about me? I have a blade for a hand.
Nice to meet you. Let's bump!
OUCH!
GAME OVER
Ready for another game?
>> Oops.

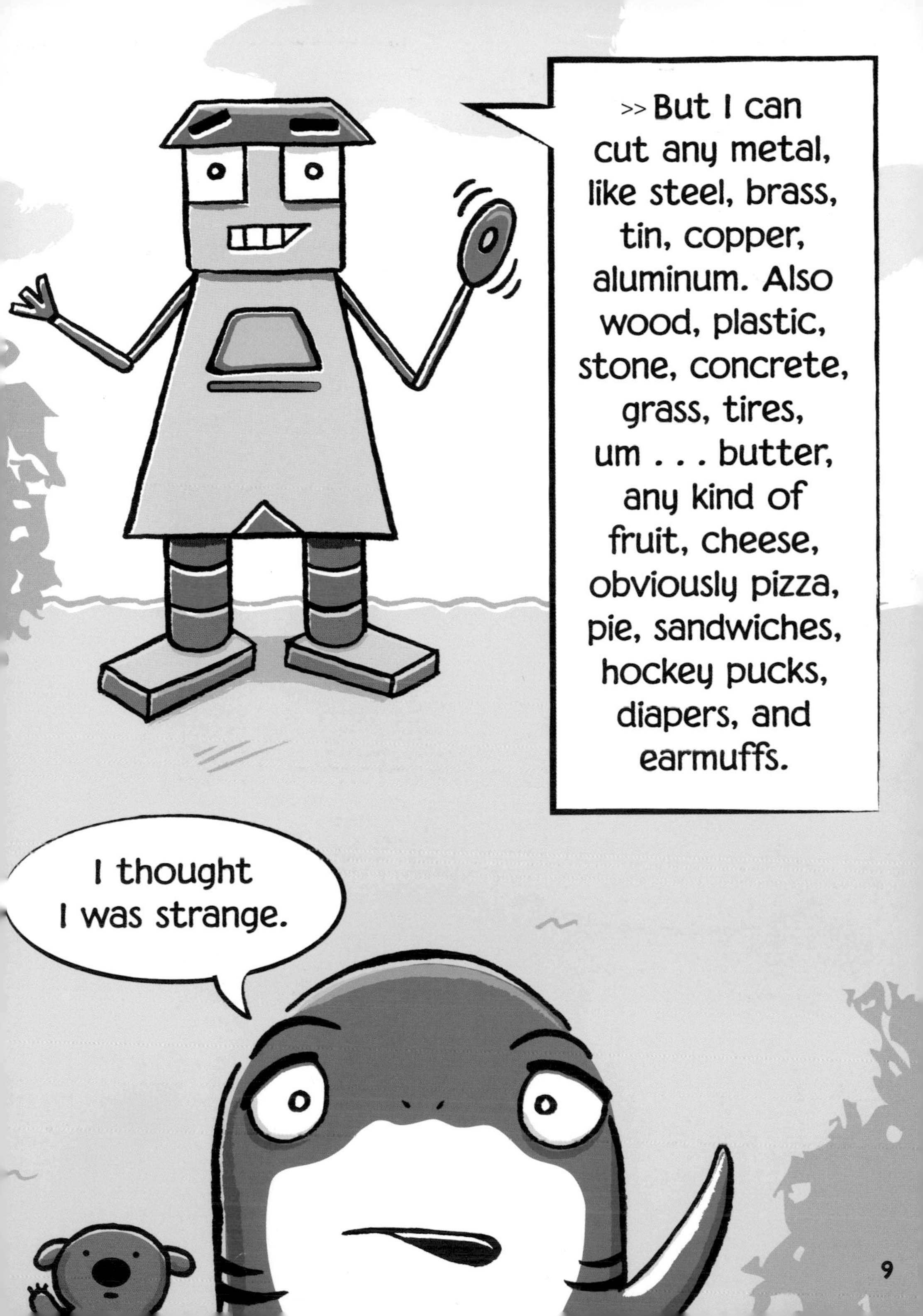
>> But I can cut any metal, like steel, brass, tin, copper, aluminum. Also wood, plastic, stone, concrete, grass, tires, um . . . butter, any kind of fruit, cheese, obviously pizza, pie, sandwiches, hockey pucks, diapers, and earmuffs.
I thought I was strange.

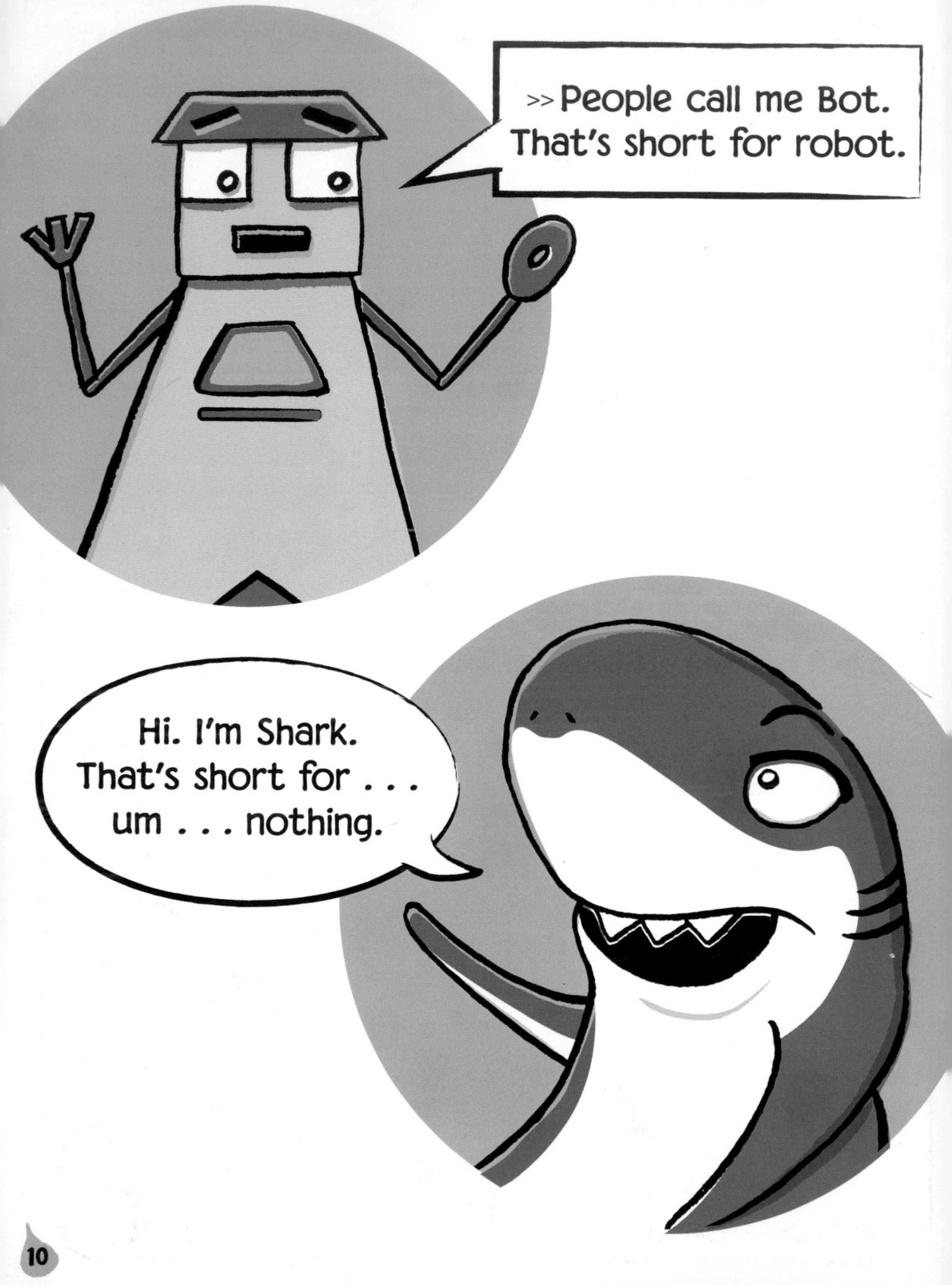
>> People call me Bot. That's short for robot.
Hi. I'm Shark. That's short for . . . um . . . nothing.

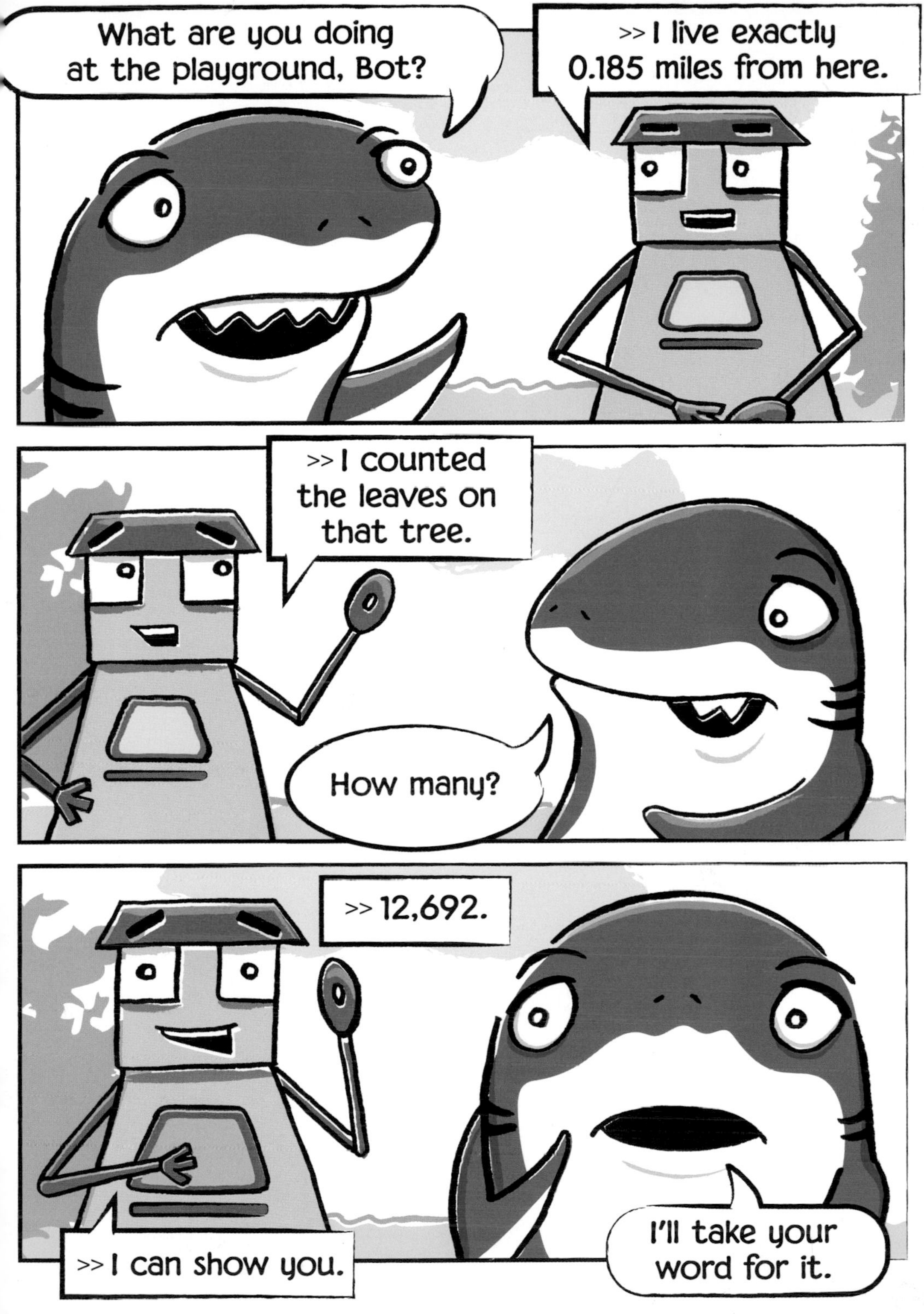
What are you doing at the playground, Bot?
>> I live exactly 0.185 miles from here.
>> I counted the leaves on that tree.
How many?
>> 12,692.
>> I can show you.
I'll take your word for it.

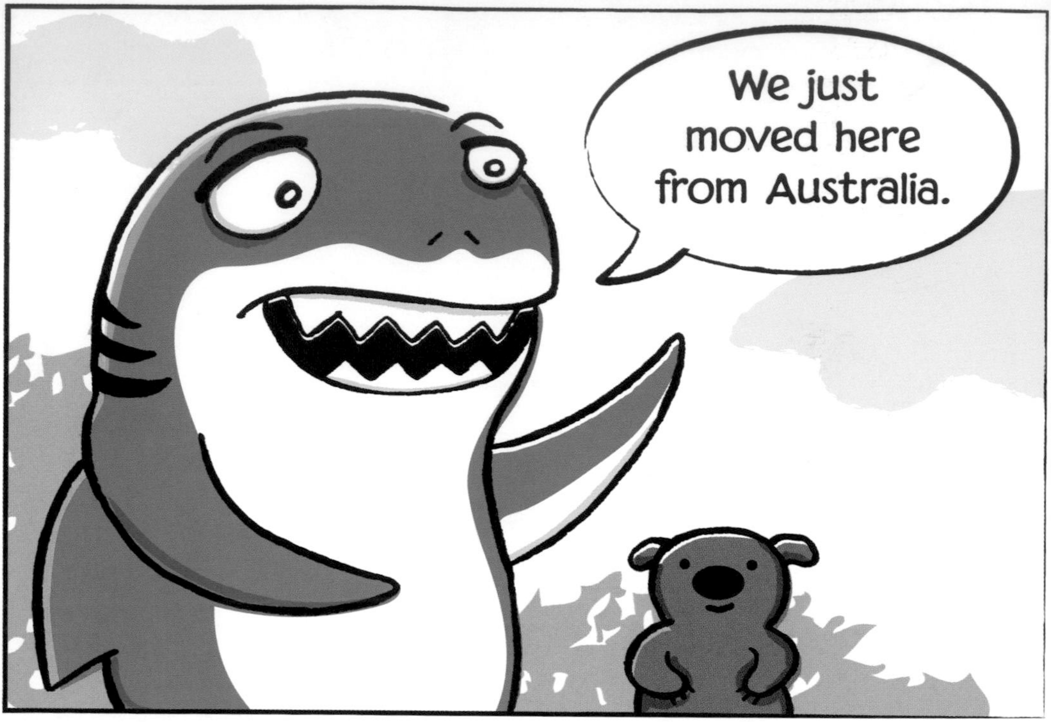
We just moved here from Australia.

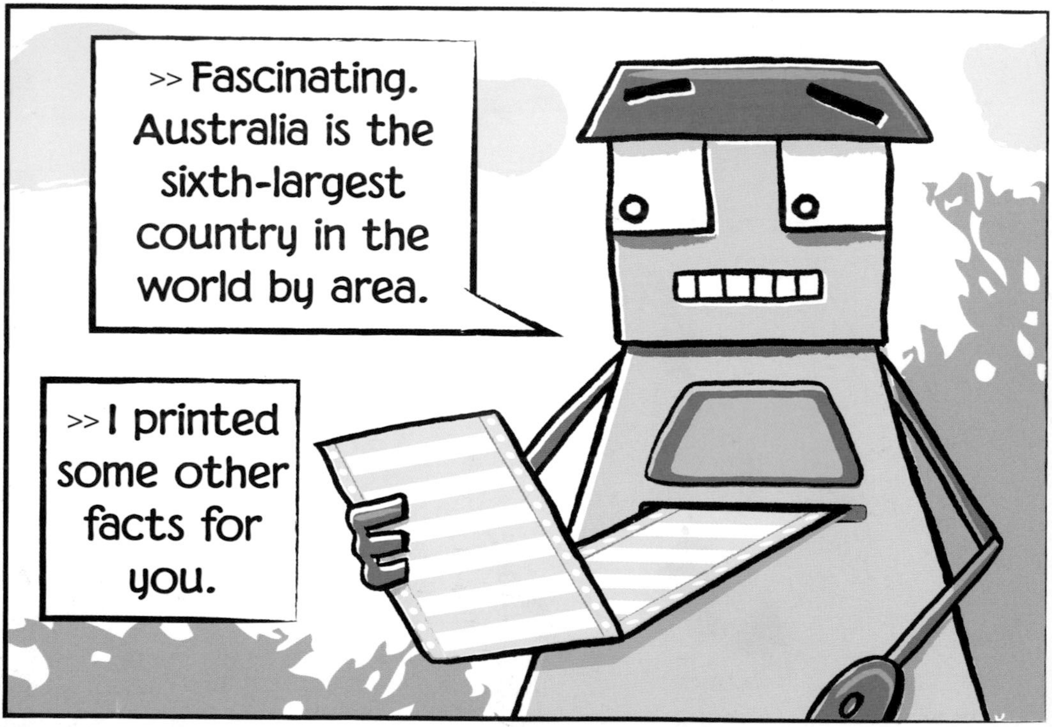
>> Fascinating. Australia is the sixth-largest country in the world by area.
>> I printed some other facts for you.

FACTS ABOUT AUSTRALIA

by BOT

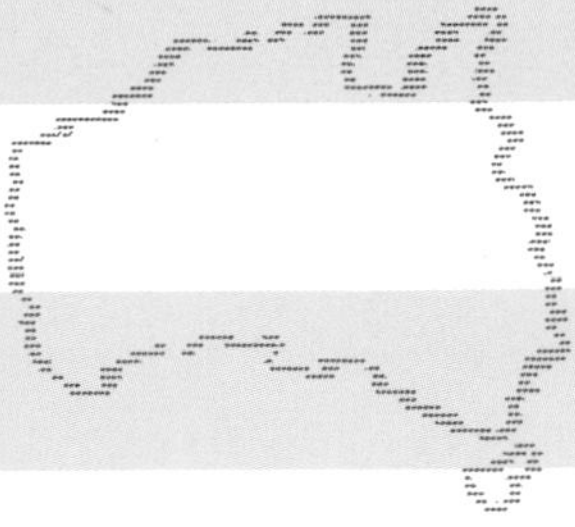

◇ Highway 1 is the longest national highway in the world. (It travels 14,500 kilometers around the whole country.)

◇ There is a mountain named Mount Disappointment. (The view is terrible.)

◇ Some of the world's most deadly animals live in Australia. (Spiders, snakes & more!)

◇ Australia has over 10,000 beaches. (Surf's up!)

◇ The first people living in Australia (the Aboriginal people) have been there for 50,000 years!

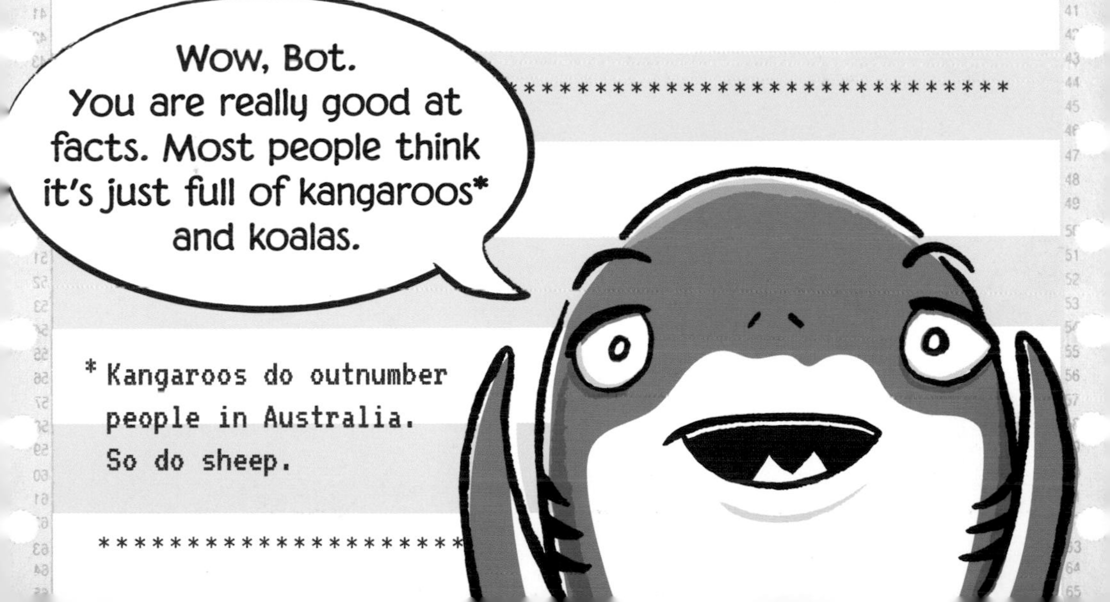

Wow, Bot.
You are really good at facts. Most people think it's just full of kangaroos* and koalas.

* Kangaroos do outnumber people in Australia. So do sheep.

Chapter 2

Us Friends?

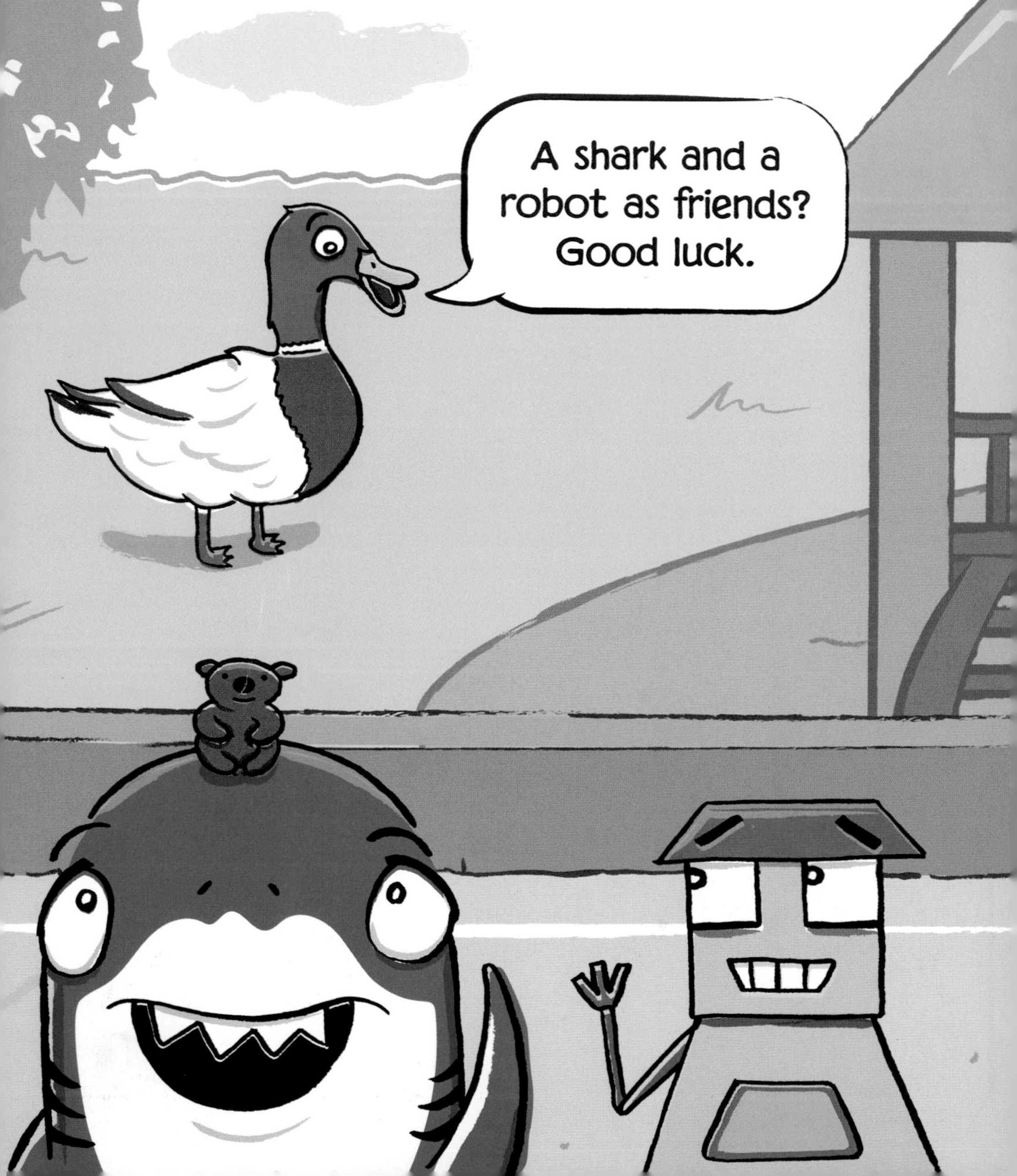
A shark and a robot as friends? Good luck.

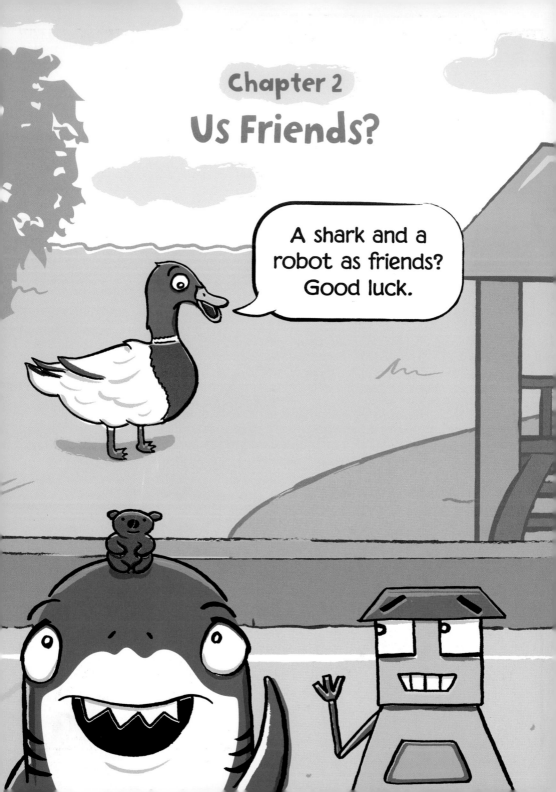

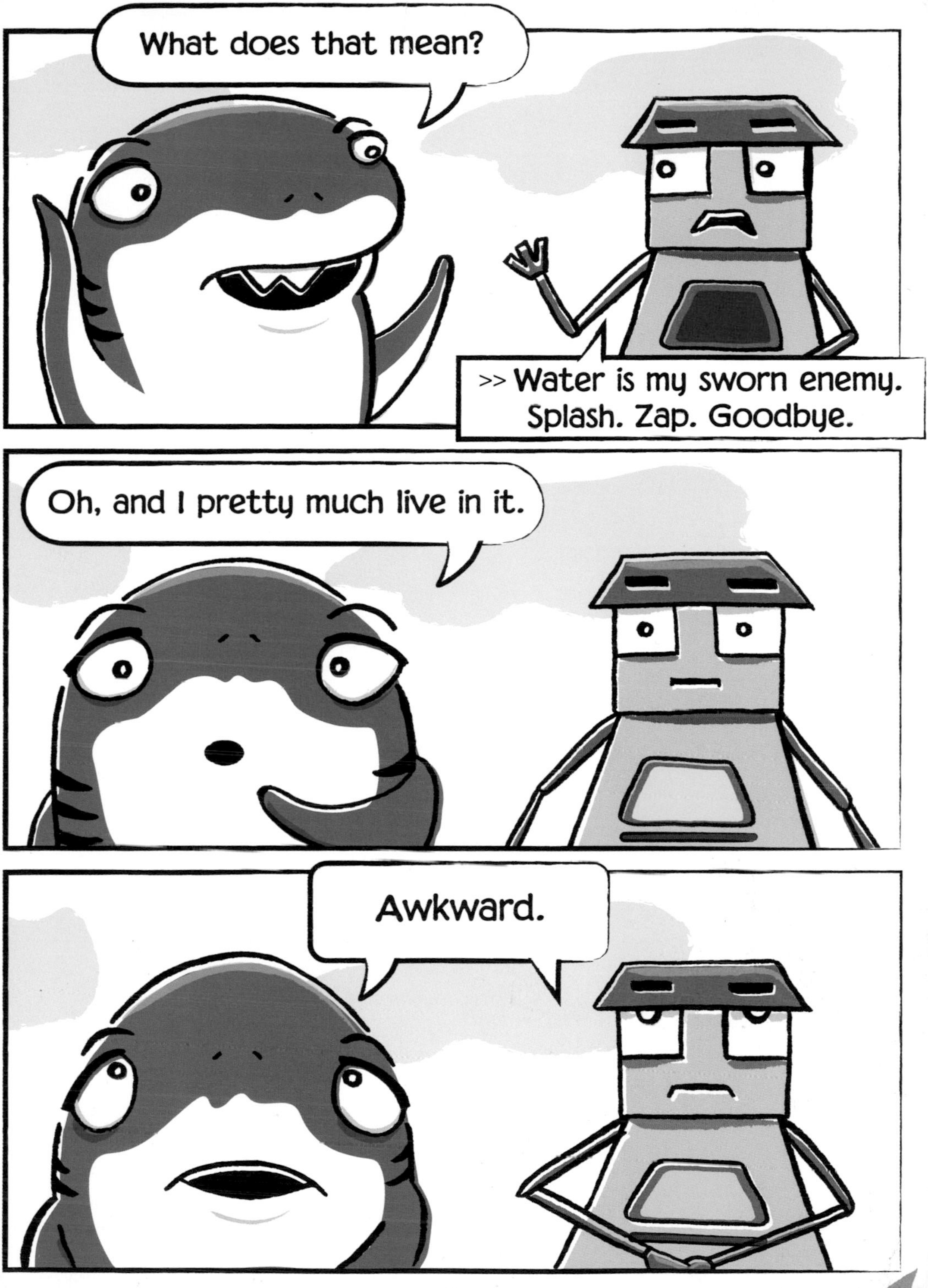
What does that mean?
>> Water is my sworn enemy. Splash. Zap. Goodbye.
Oh, and I pretty much live in it.
Awkward.

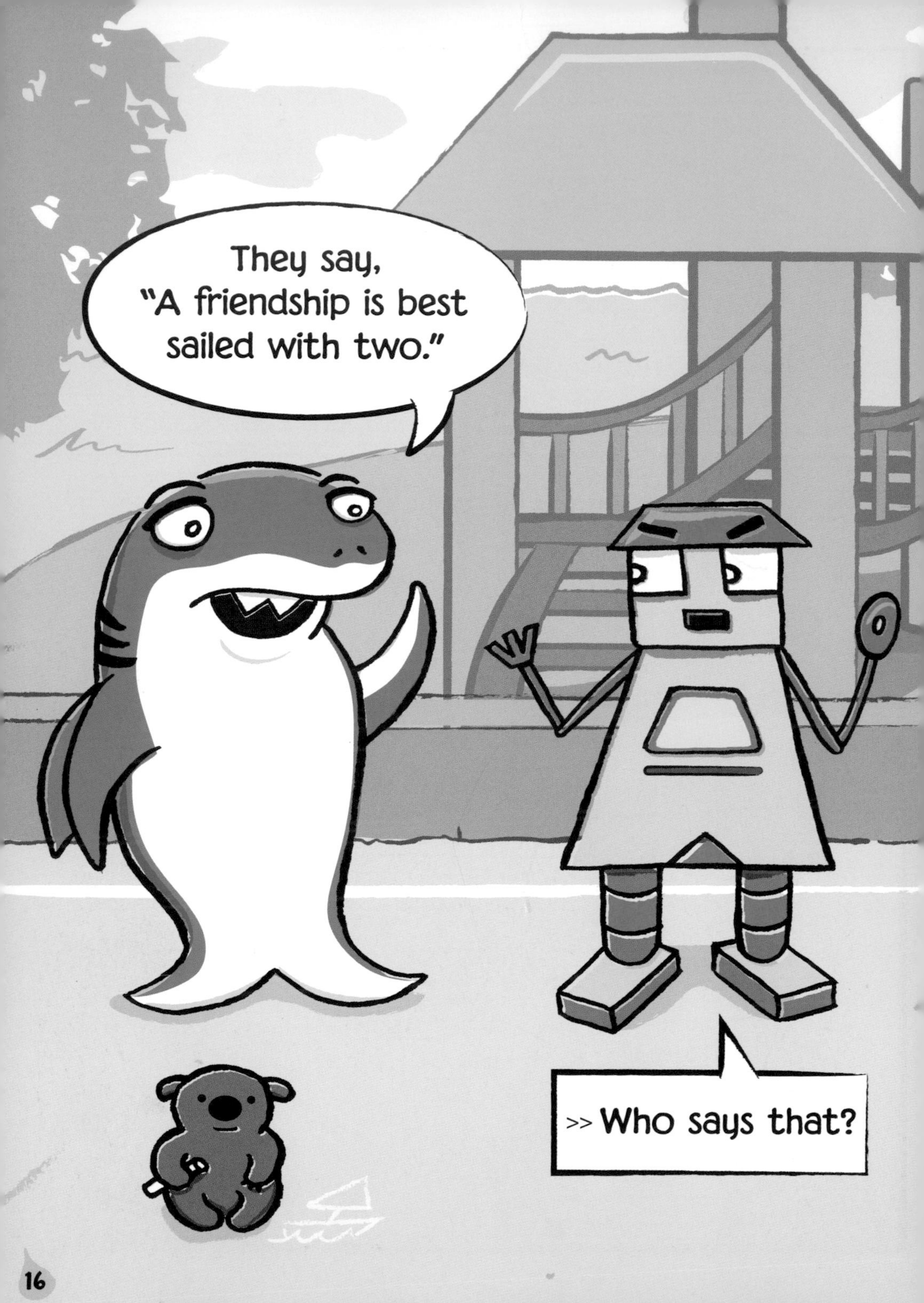
They say,
"A friendship is best sailed with two."
>> Who says that?

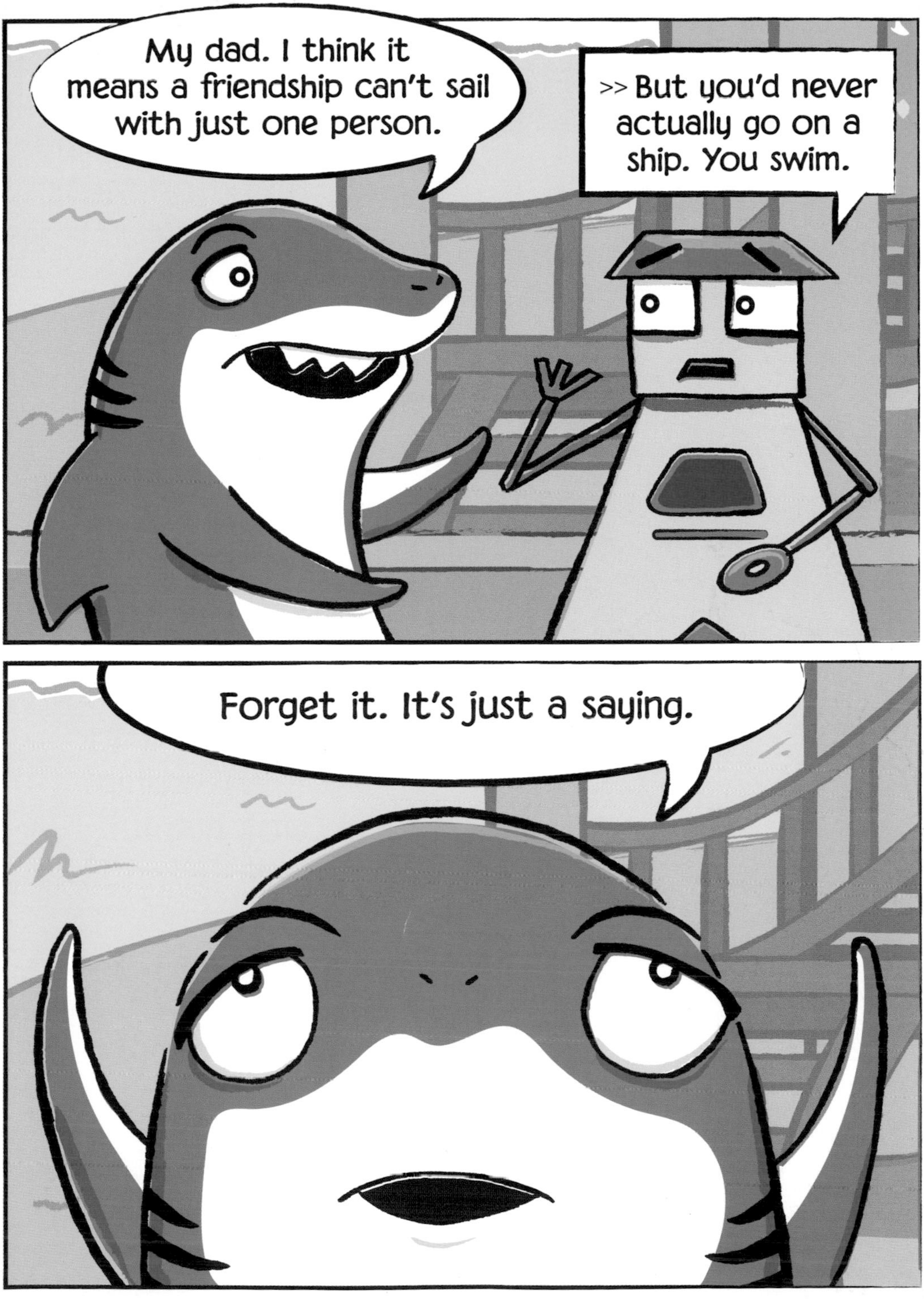
My dad. I think it means a friendship can't sail with just one person.
>> But you'd never actually go on a ship. You swim.
Forget it. It's just a saying.

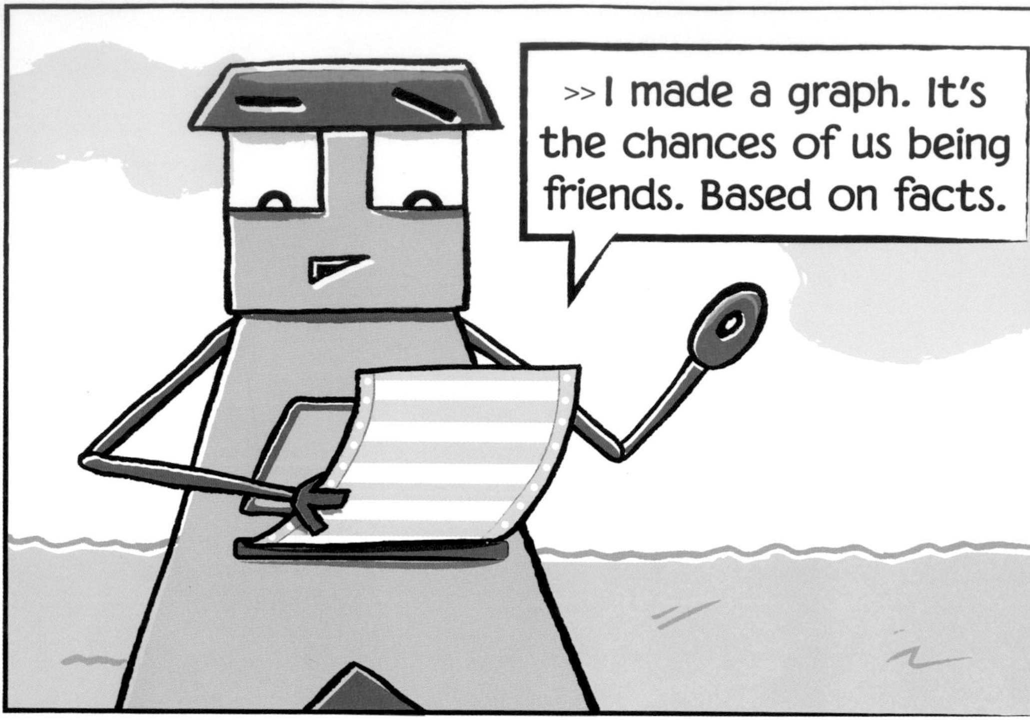
>> I made a graph. It's the chances of us being friends. Based on facts.

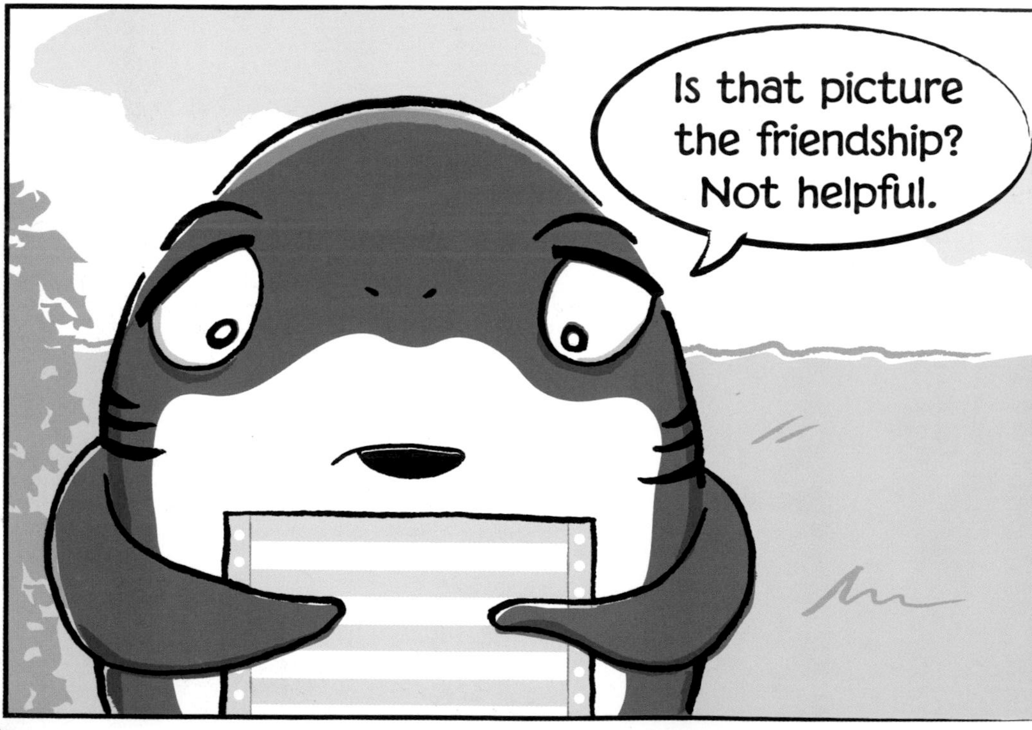
Is that picture the friendship? Not helpful.

THINGS THAT GO TOGETHER

by BOT

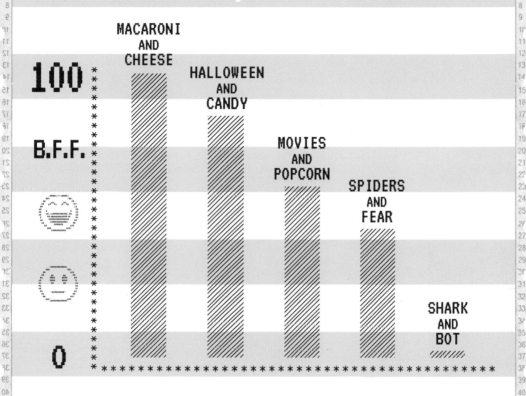

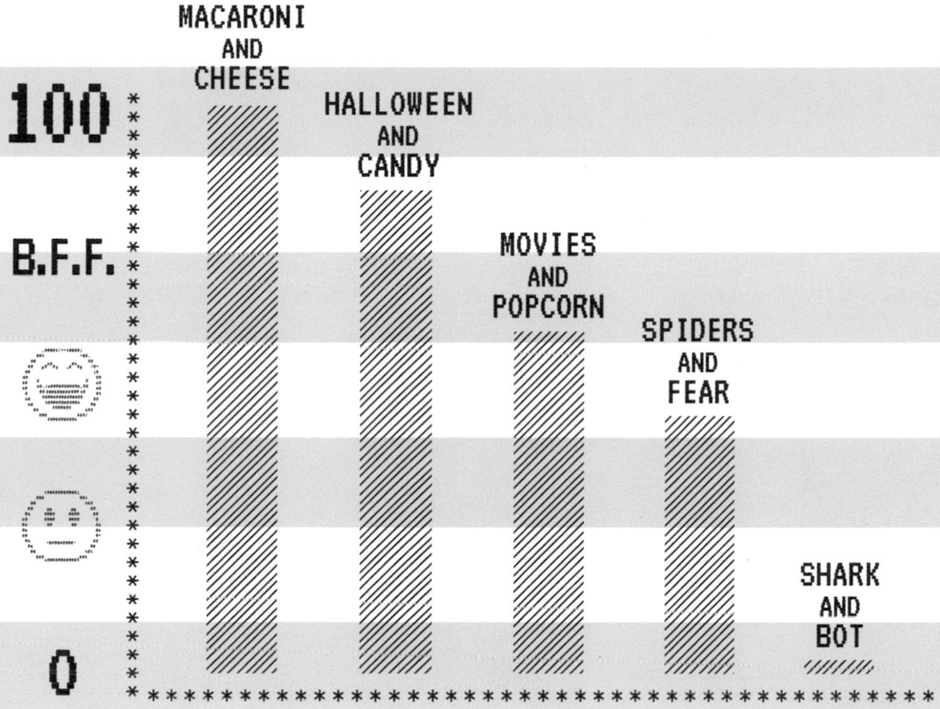
100
B.F.F.
0
MACARONI AND CHEESE
HALLOWEEN AND CANDY
MOVIES AND POPCORN
SPIDERS AND FEAR
SHARK AND BOT

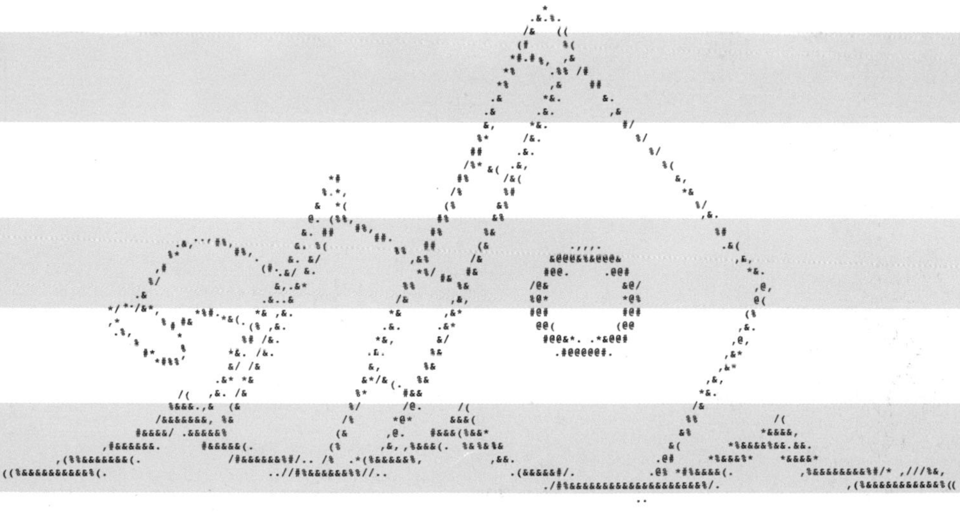

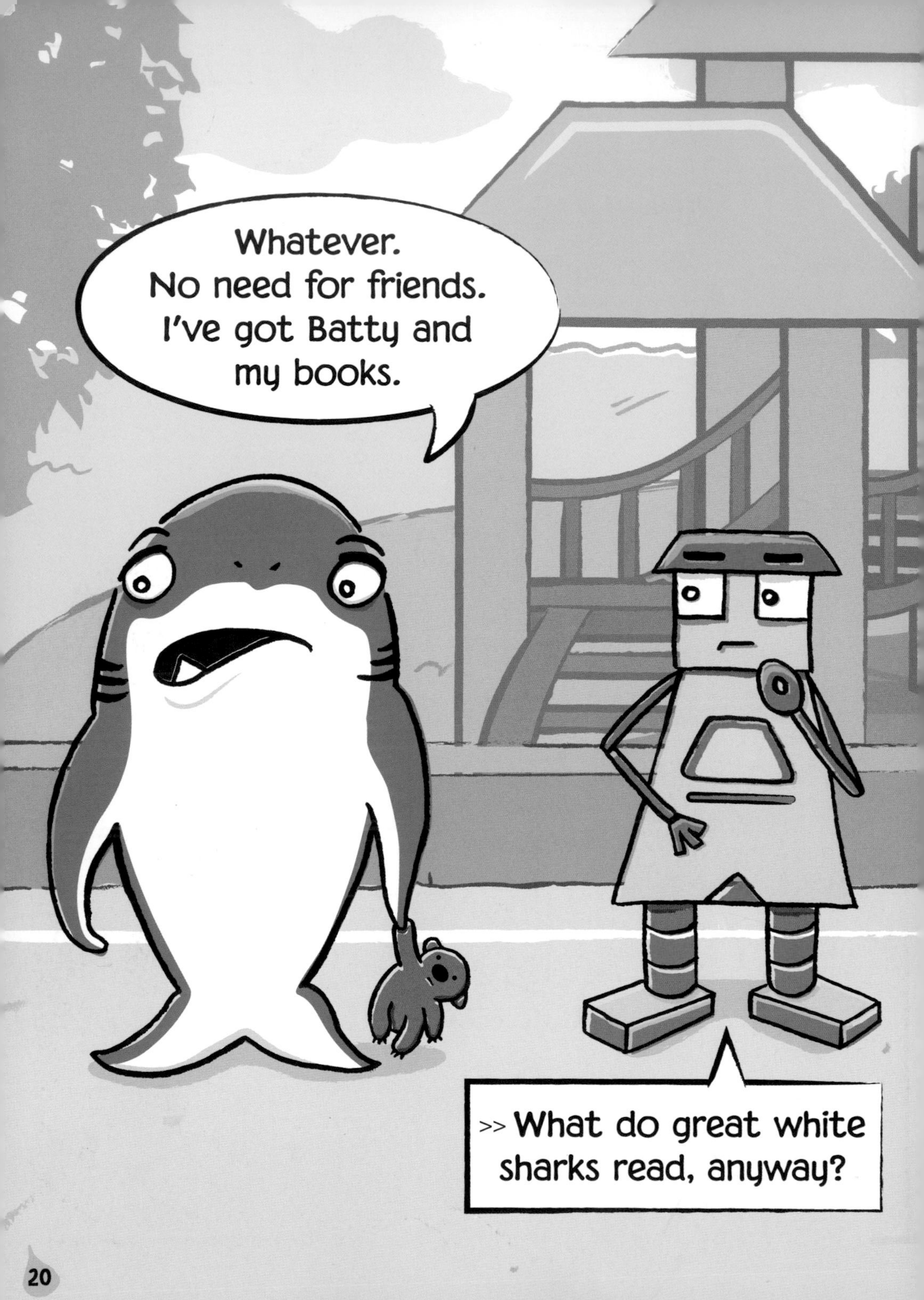
Whatever. No need for friends. I've got Batty and my books.
>> What do great white sharks read, anyway?

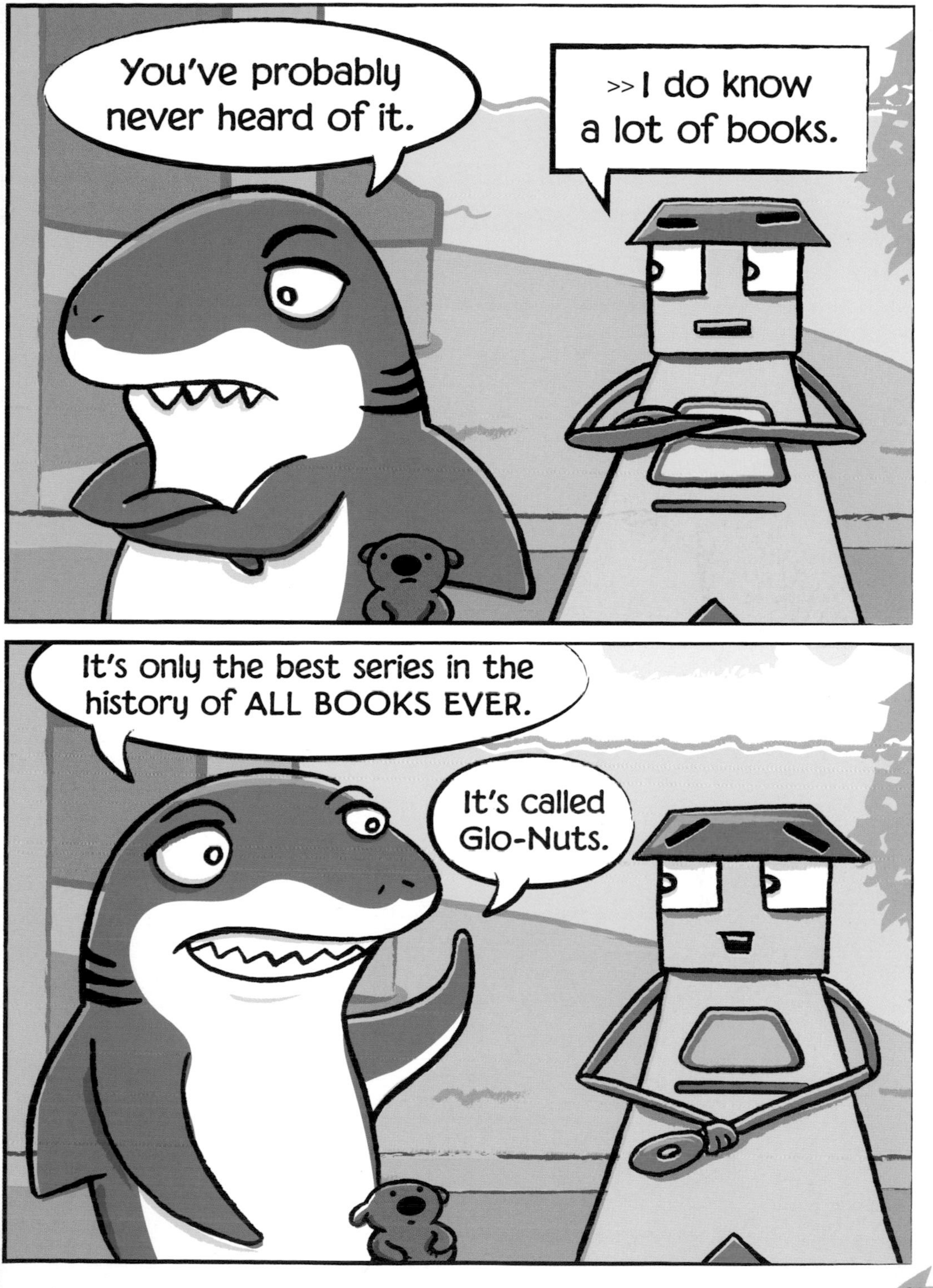

You've probably never heard of it.
>>I do know a lot of books.
It's only the best series in the history of ALL BOOKS EVER.
It's called Glo-Nuts.

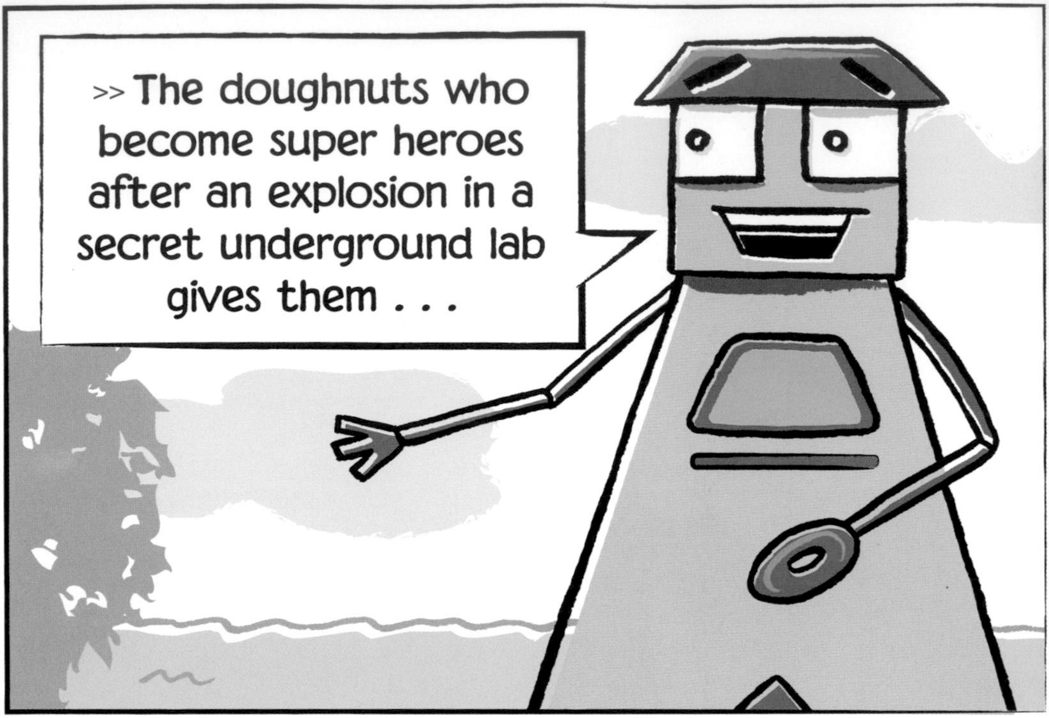
>> The doughnuts who become super heroes after an explosion in a secret underground lab gives them . . .

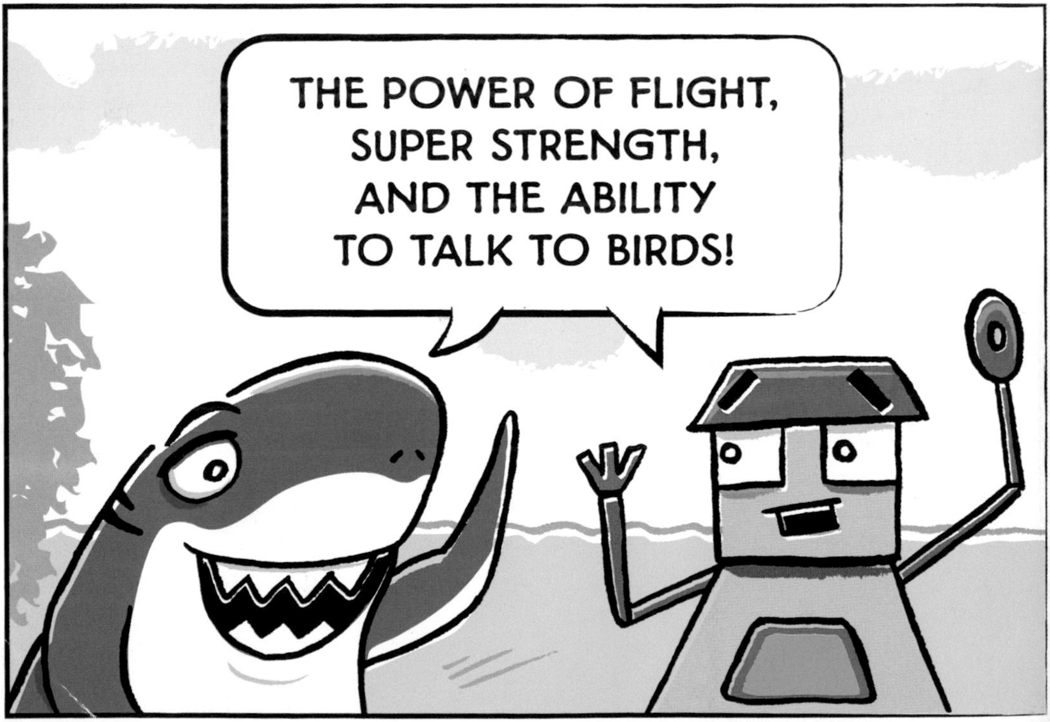
THE POWER OF FLIGHT, SUPER STRENGTH, AND THE ABILITY TO TALK TO BIRDS!

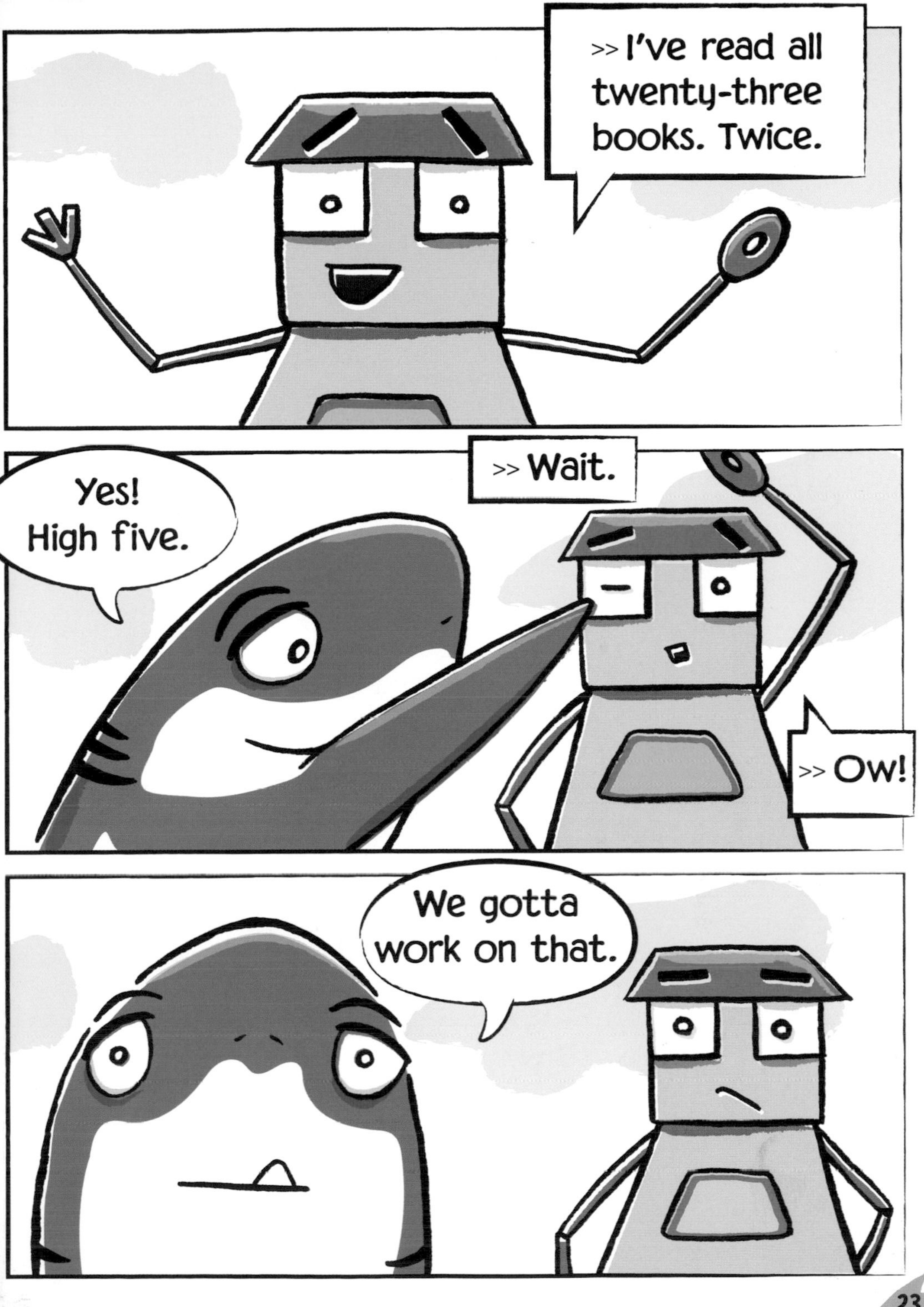
>> I've read all twenty-three books. Twice.
Yes! High five.
>> Wait.
>> Ow!
We gotta work on that.

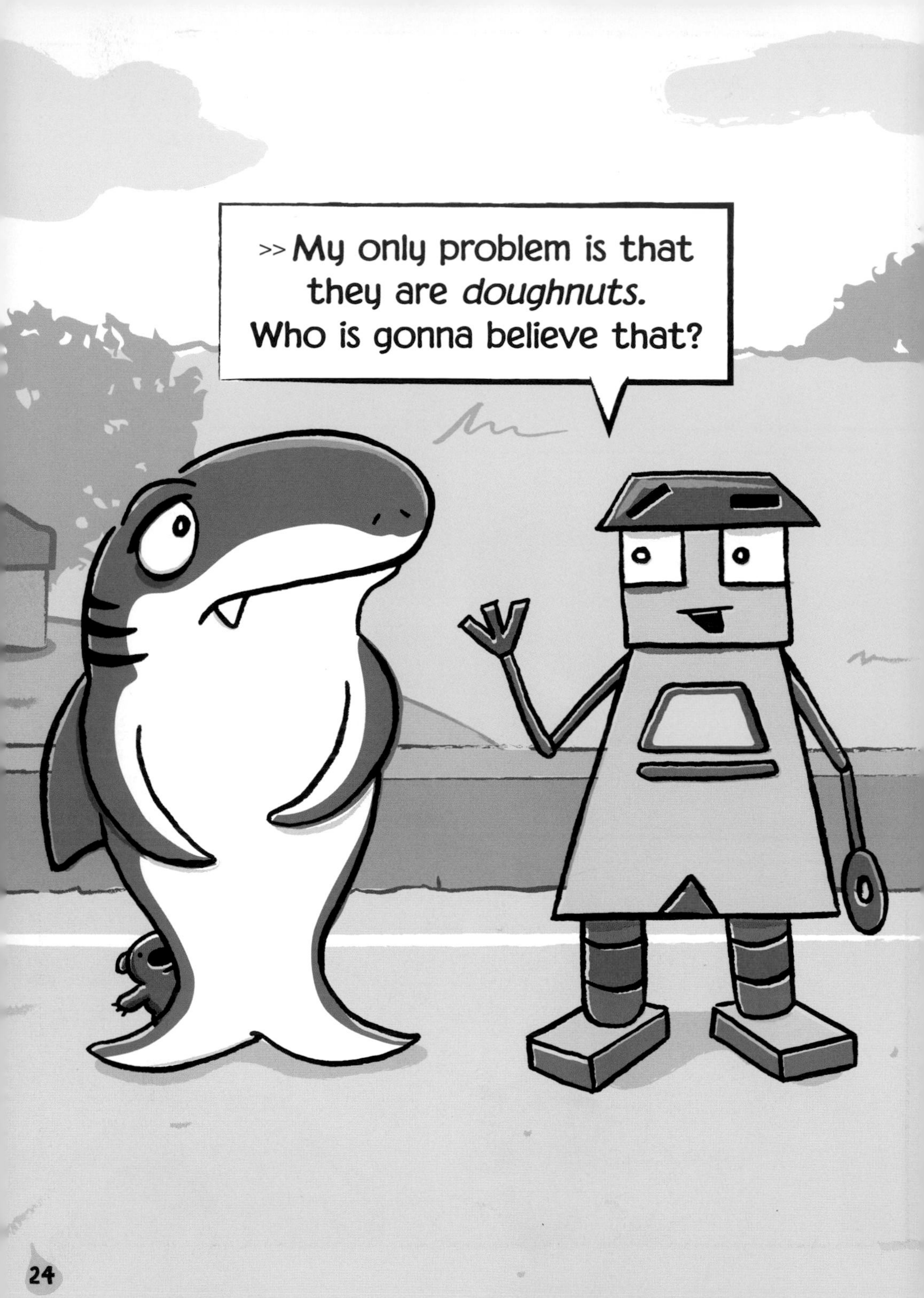
>> My only problem is that they are *doughnuts.* Who is gonna believe that?

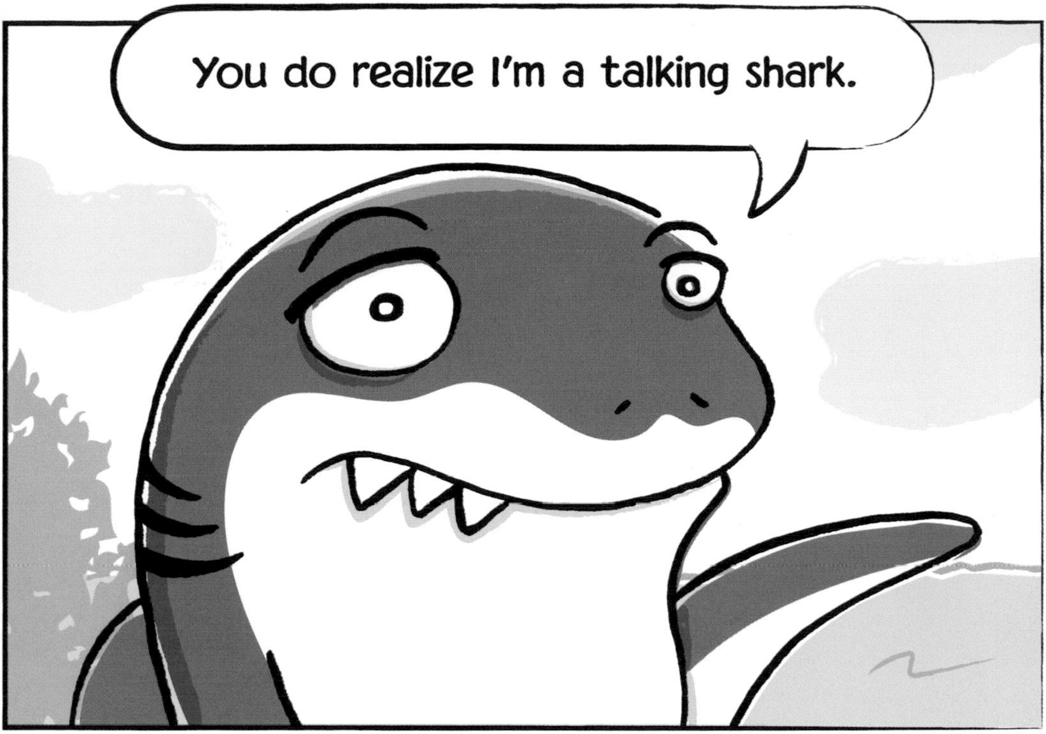
You do realize I'm a talking shark.

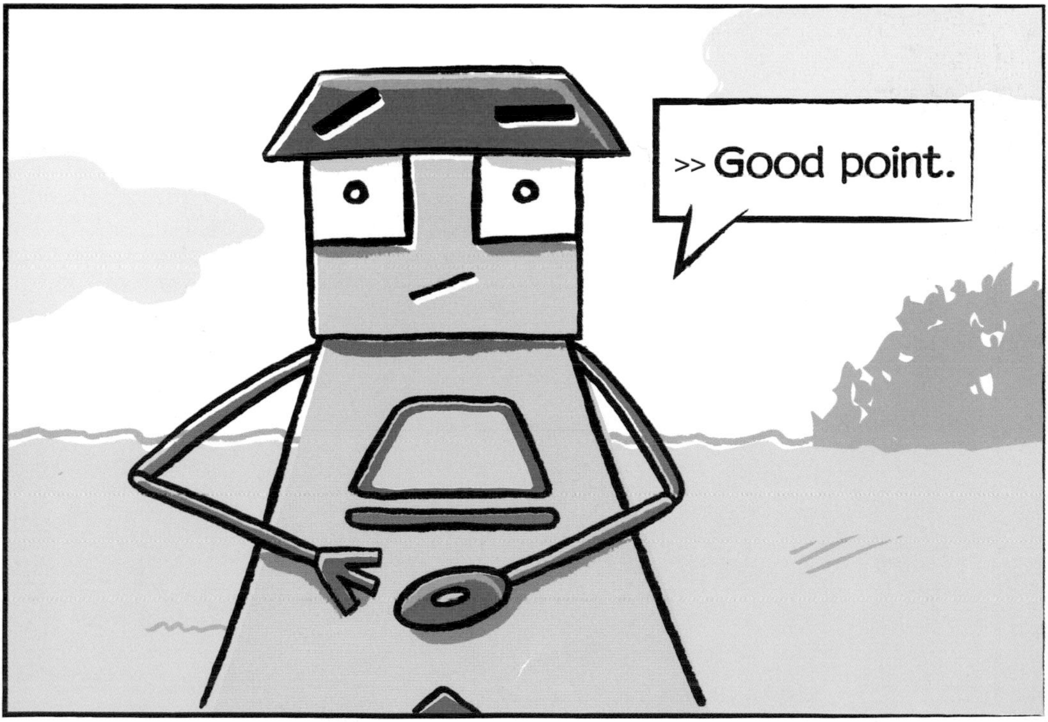
>> Good point.

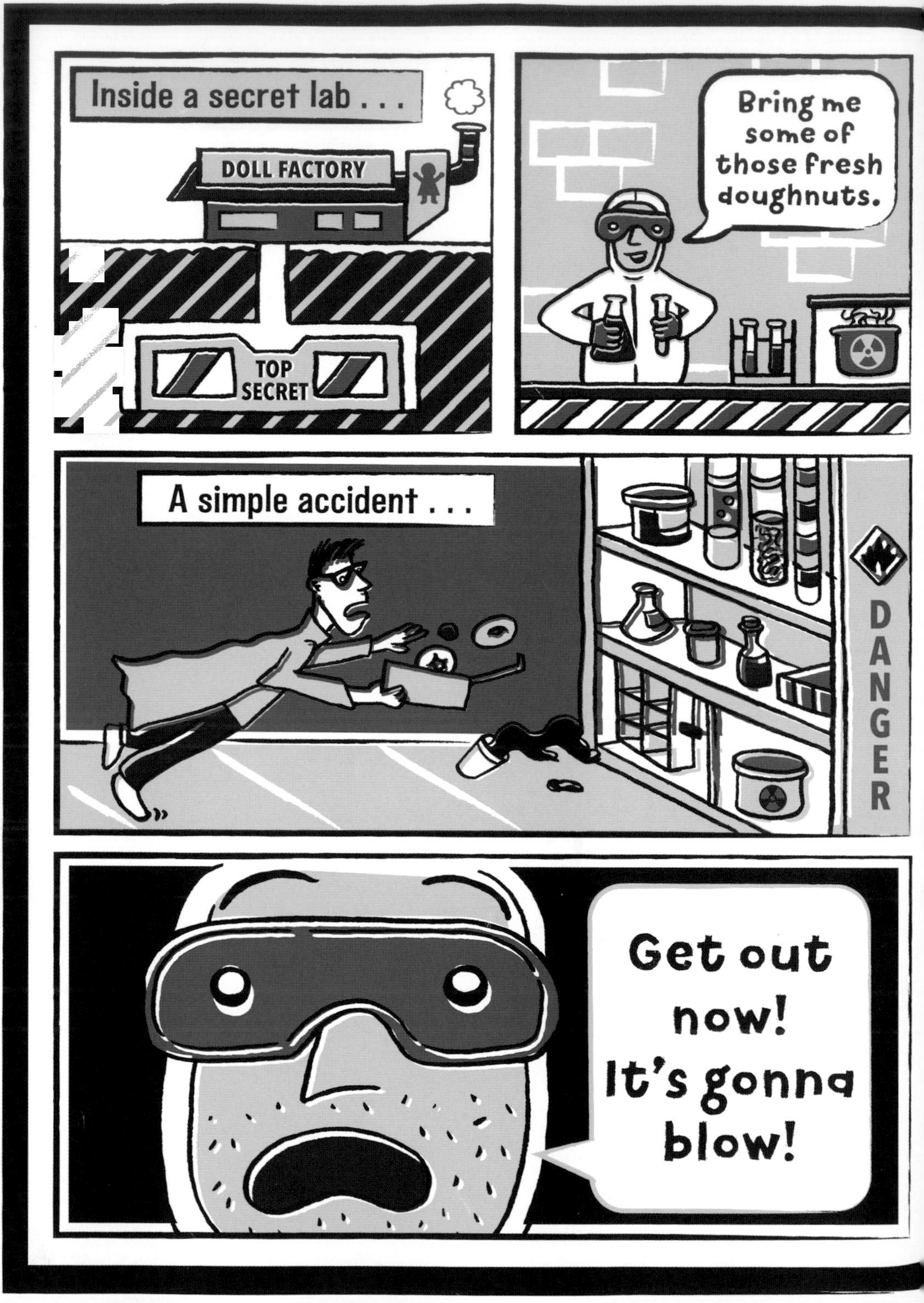
Inside a secret lab . . .
DOLL FACTORY
TOP SECRET
Bring me some of those fresh doughnuts.
A simple accident . . .
DANGER
Get out now! It's gonna blow!

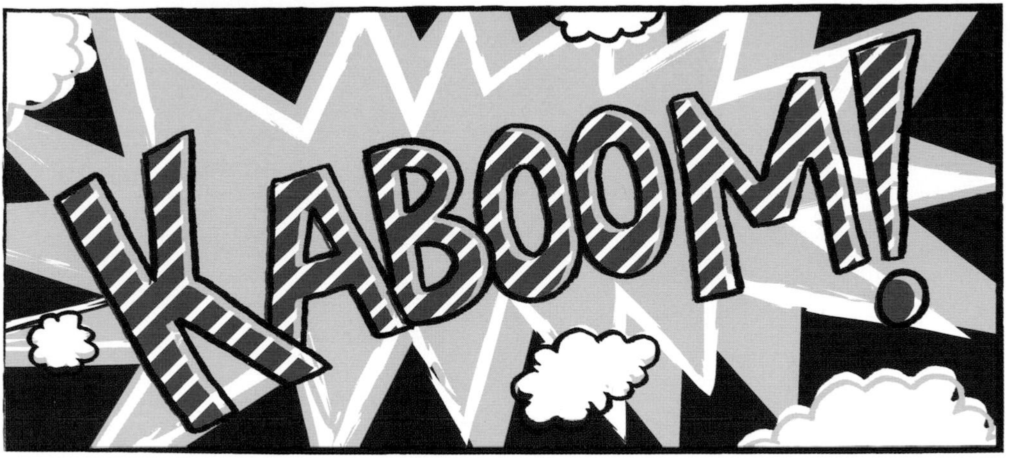
KABOOM!

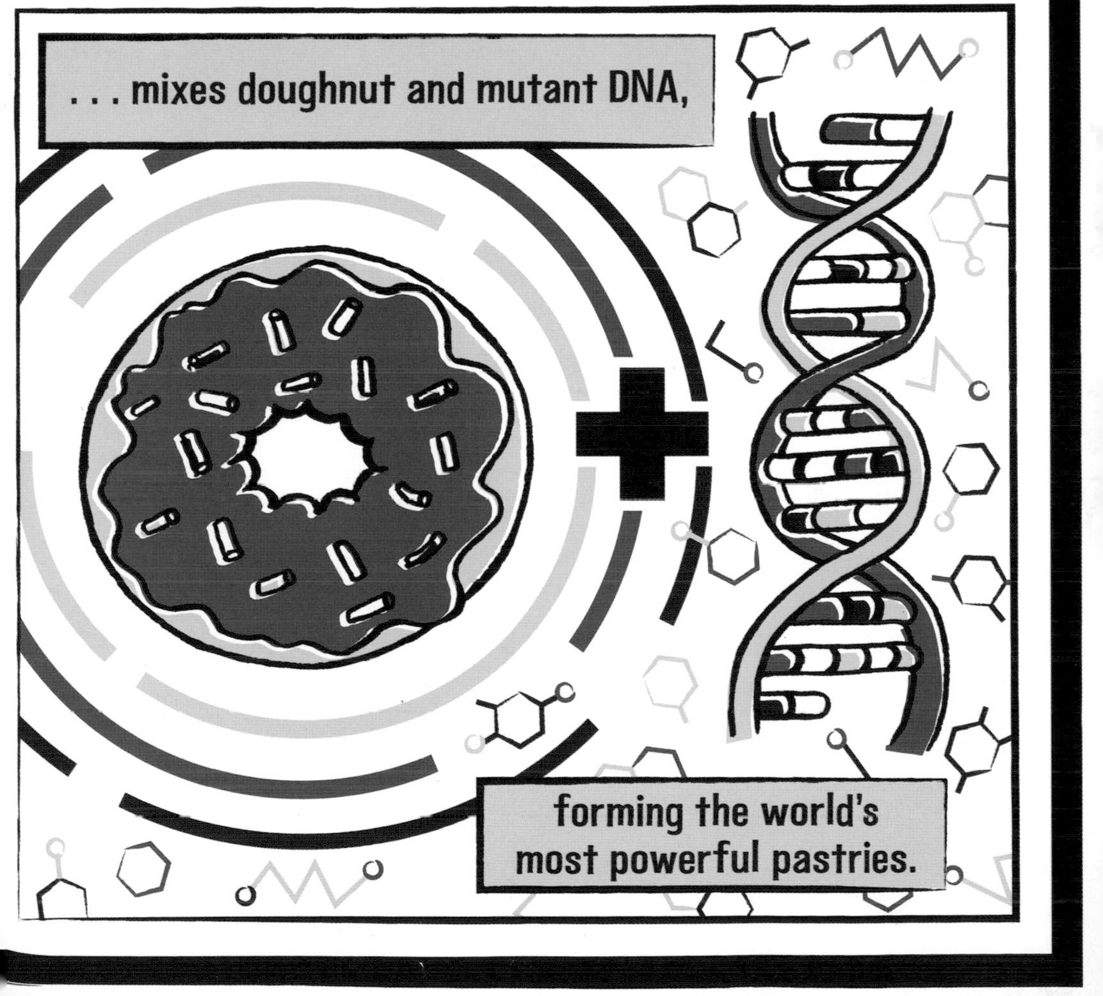
. . . mixes doughnut and mutant DNA,
forming the world's most powerful pastries.

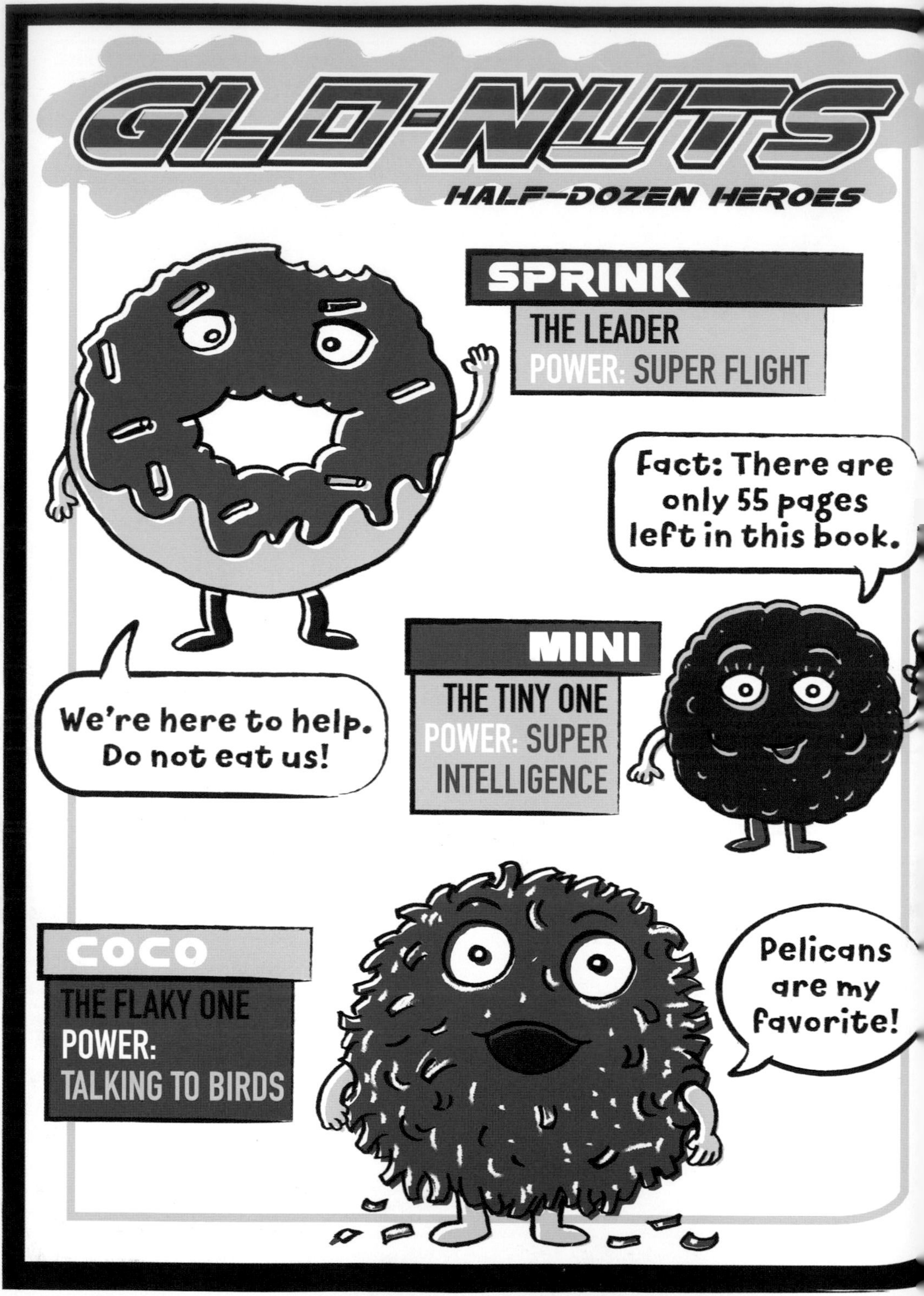
GLO-NUTS
HALF-DOZEN HEROES
SPRINK
THE LEADER
POWER: SUPER FLIGHT
Fact: There are only 55 pages left in this book.
We're here to help. Do not eat us!
MINI
THE TINY ONE
POWER: SUPER INTELLIGENCE
COCO
THE FLAKY ONE
POWER: TALKING TO BIRDS
Pelicans are my favorite!

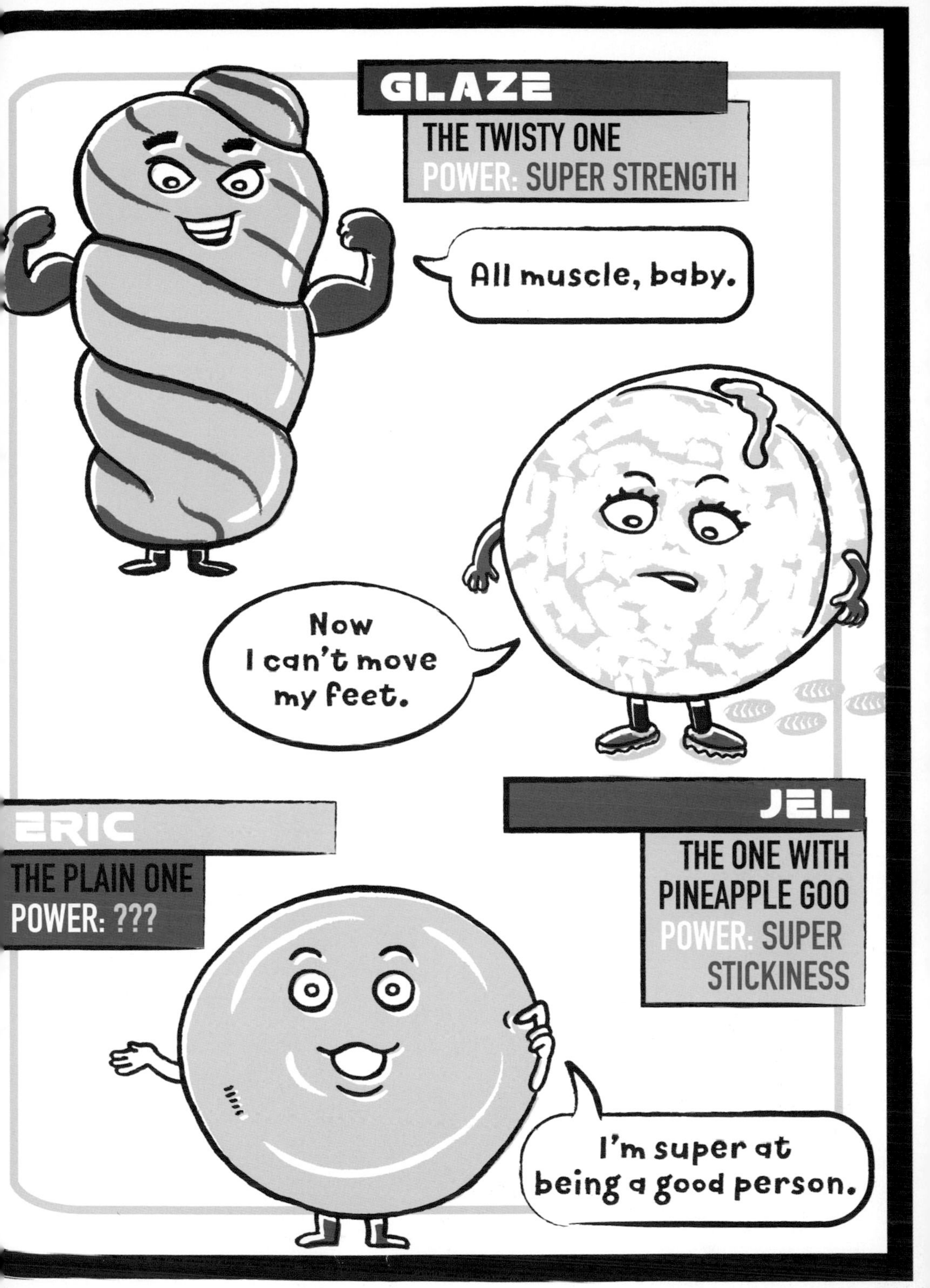
GLAZE
THE TWISTY ONE
POWER: SUPER STRENGTH
All muscle, baby.
Now I can't move my feet.
JEL
THE ONE WITH PINEAPPLE GOO
POWER: SUPER STICKINESS
ERIC
THE PLAIN ONE
POWER: ???
I'm super at being a good person.

Chapter 3

Stand Your Playground

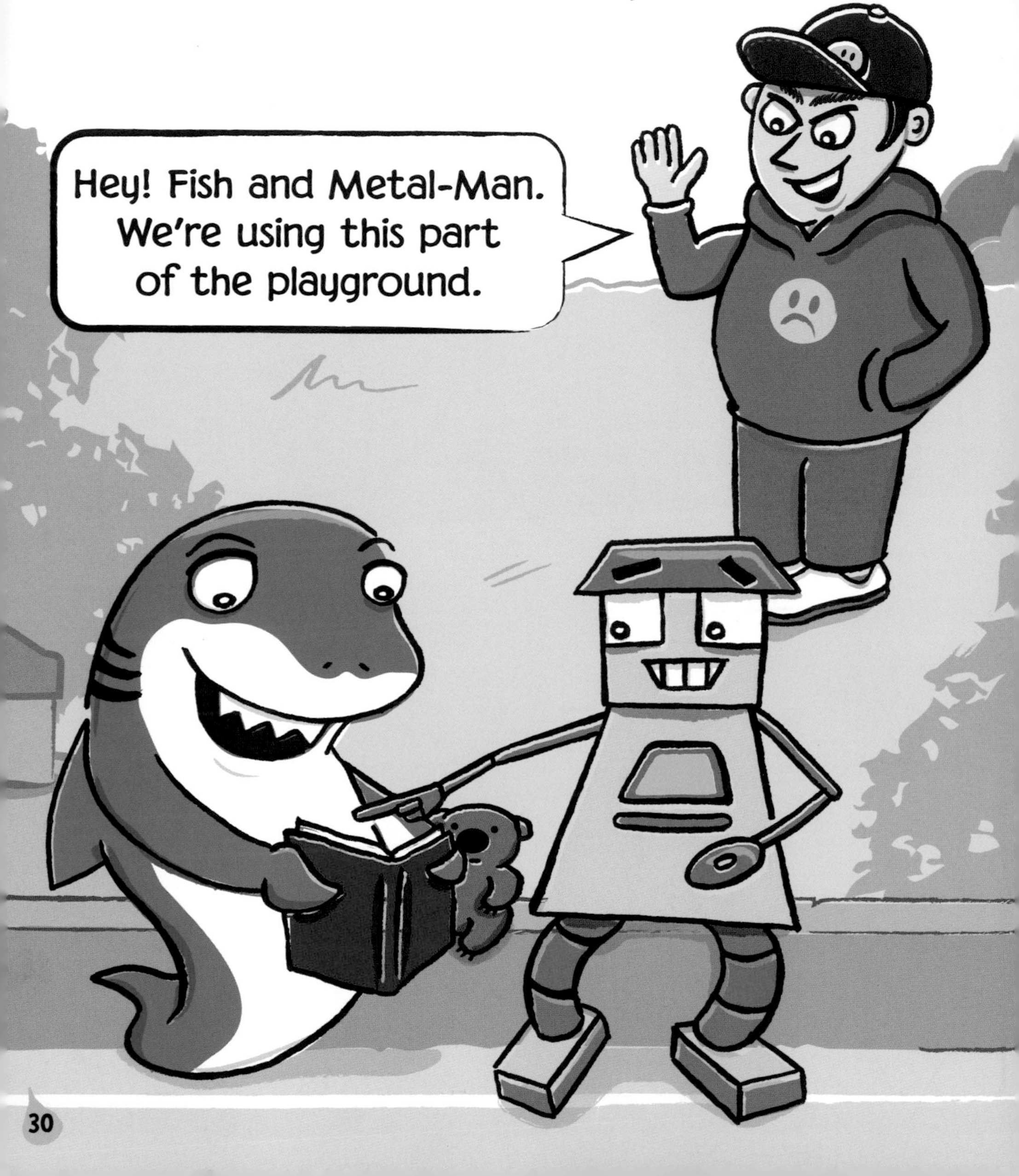
Hey! Fish and Metal-Man. We're using this part of the playground.

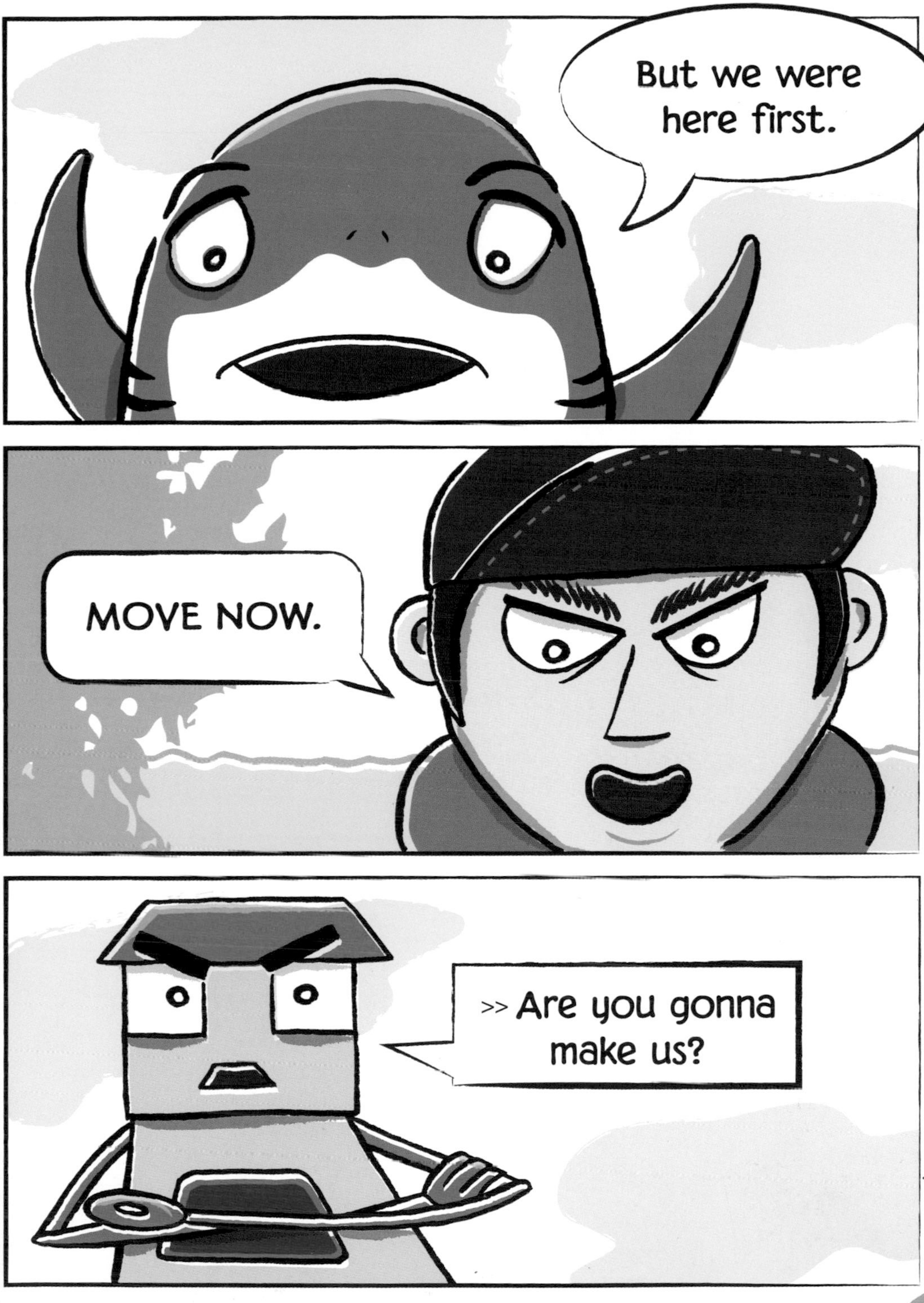
But we were here first.
MOVE NOW.
>> Are you gonna make us?

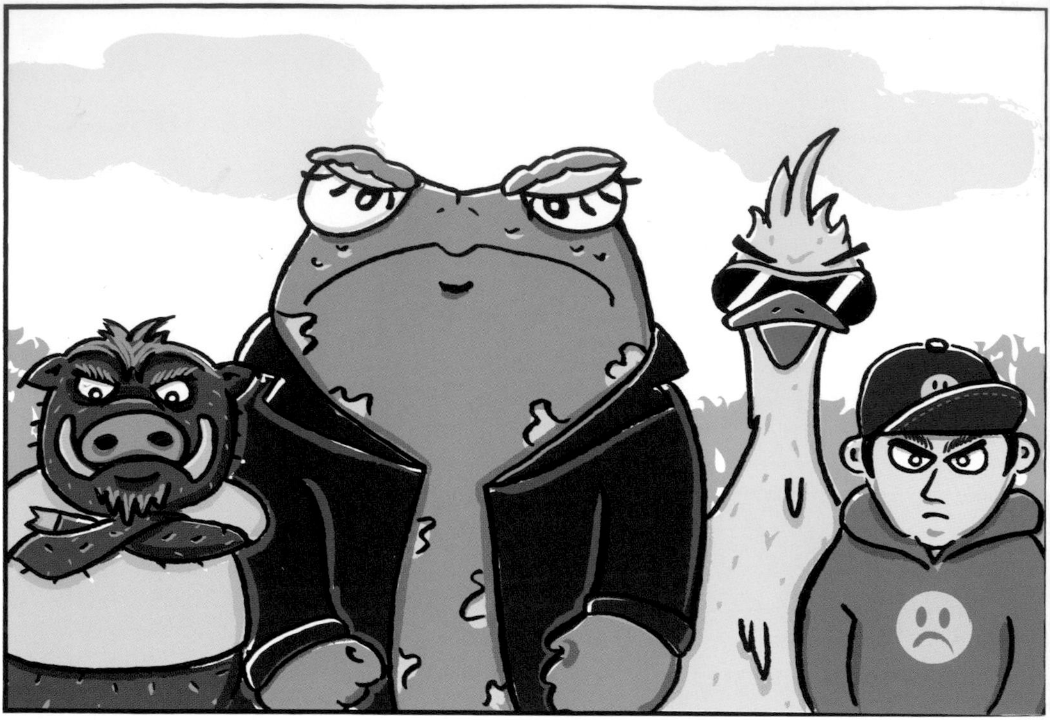

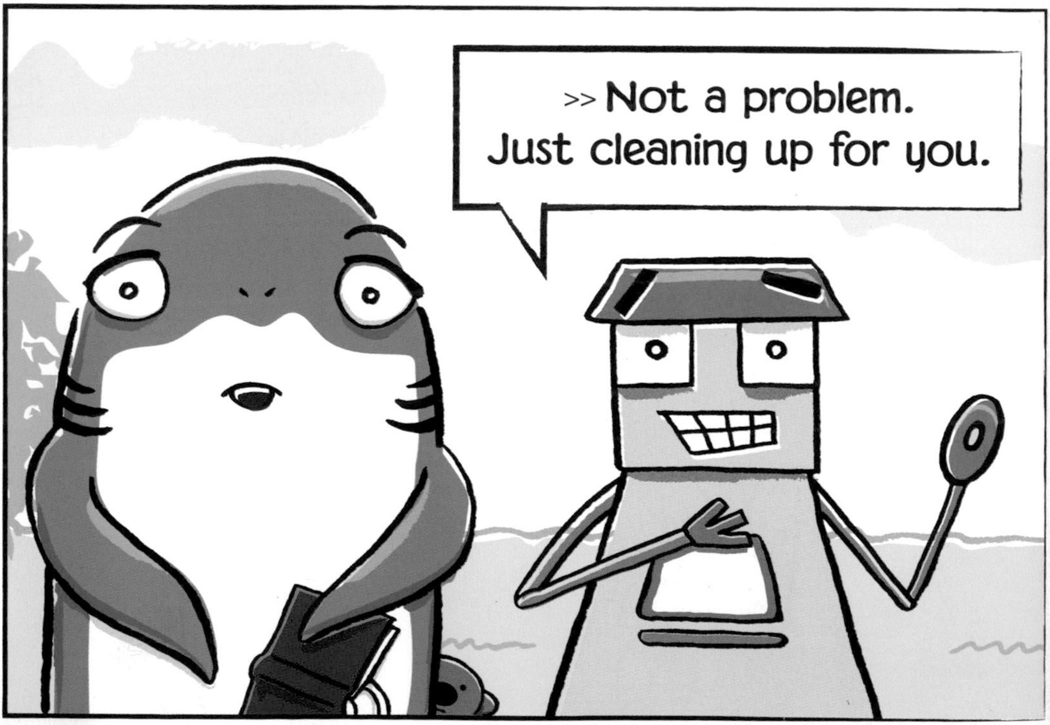
>> Not a problem.
Just cleaning up for you.

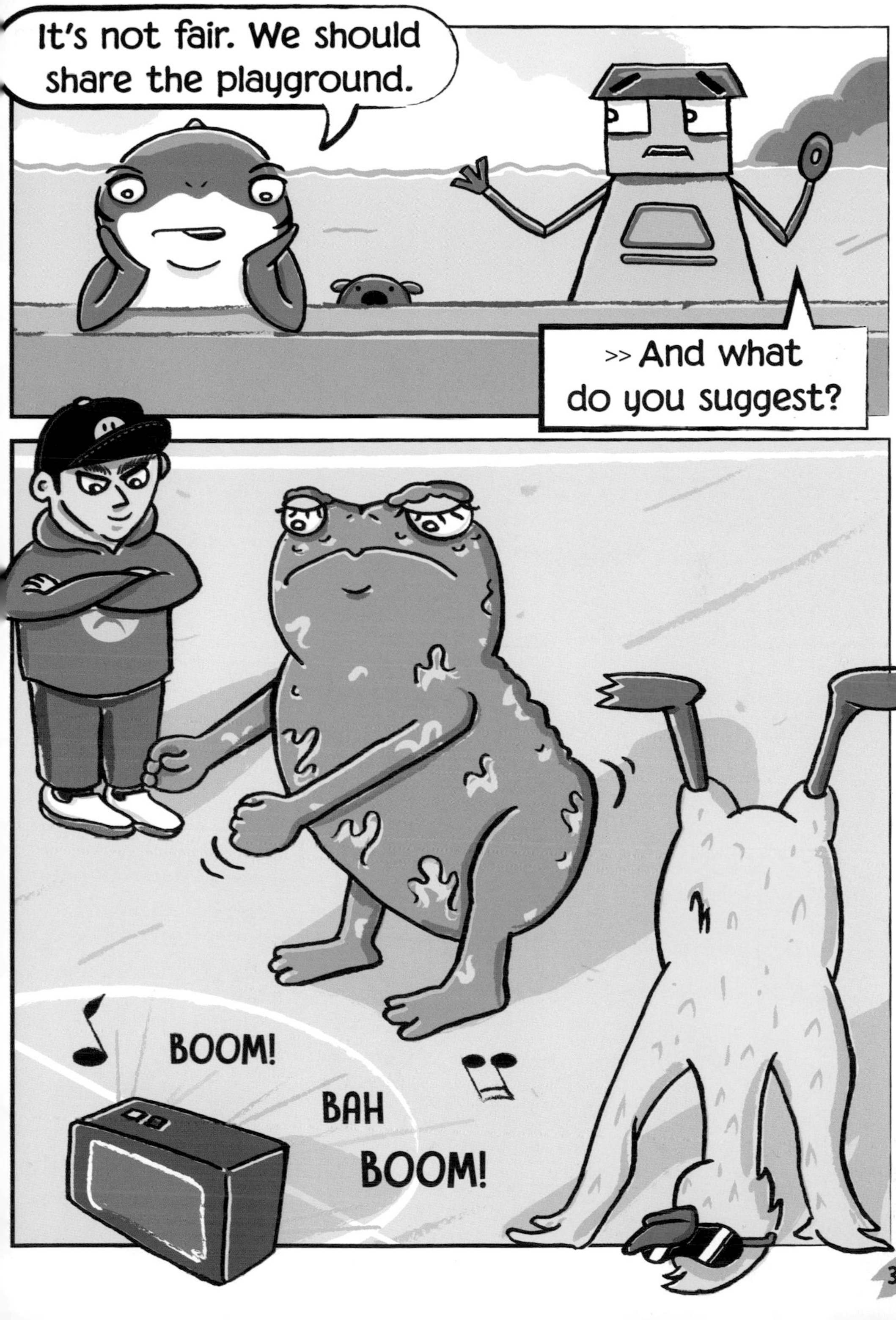
It's not fair. We should share the playground.
>> And what do you suggest?
BOOM!
BAH
BOOM!

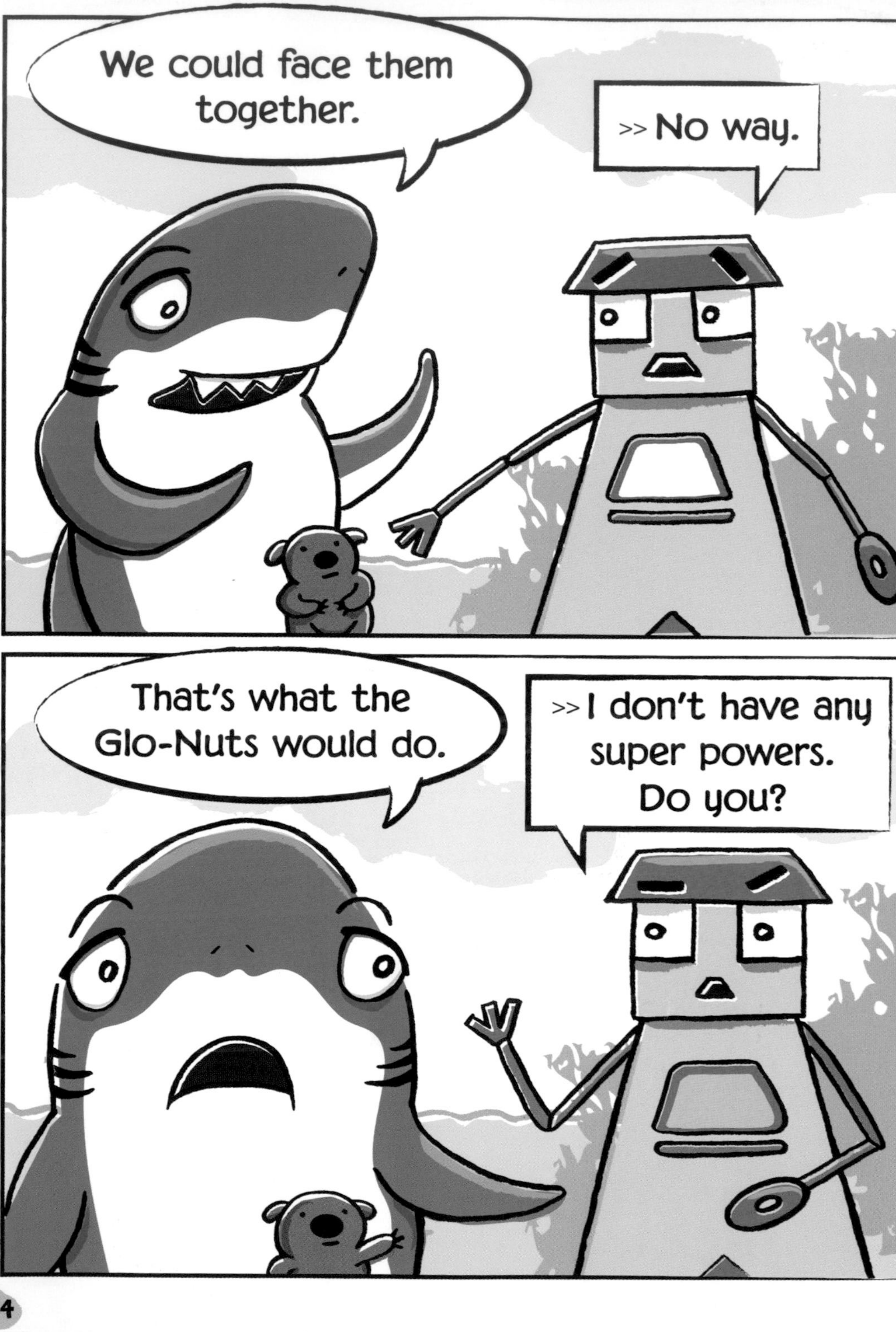
We could face them together.
>> No way.
That's what the Glo-Nuts would do.
>> I don't have any super powers. Do you?

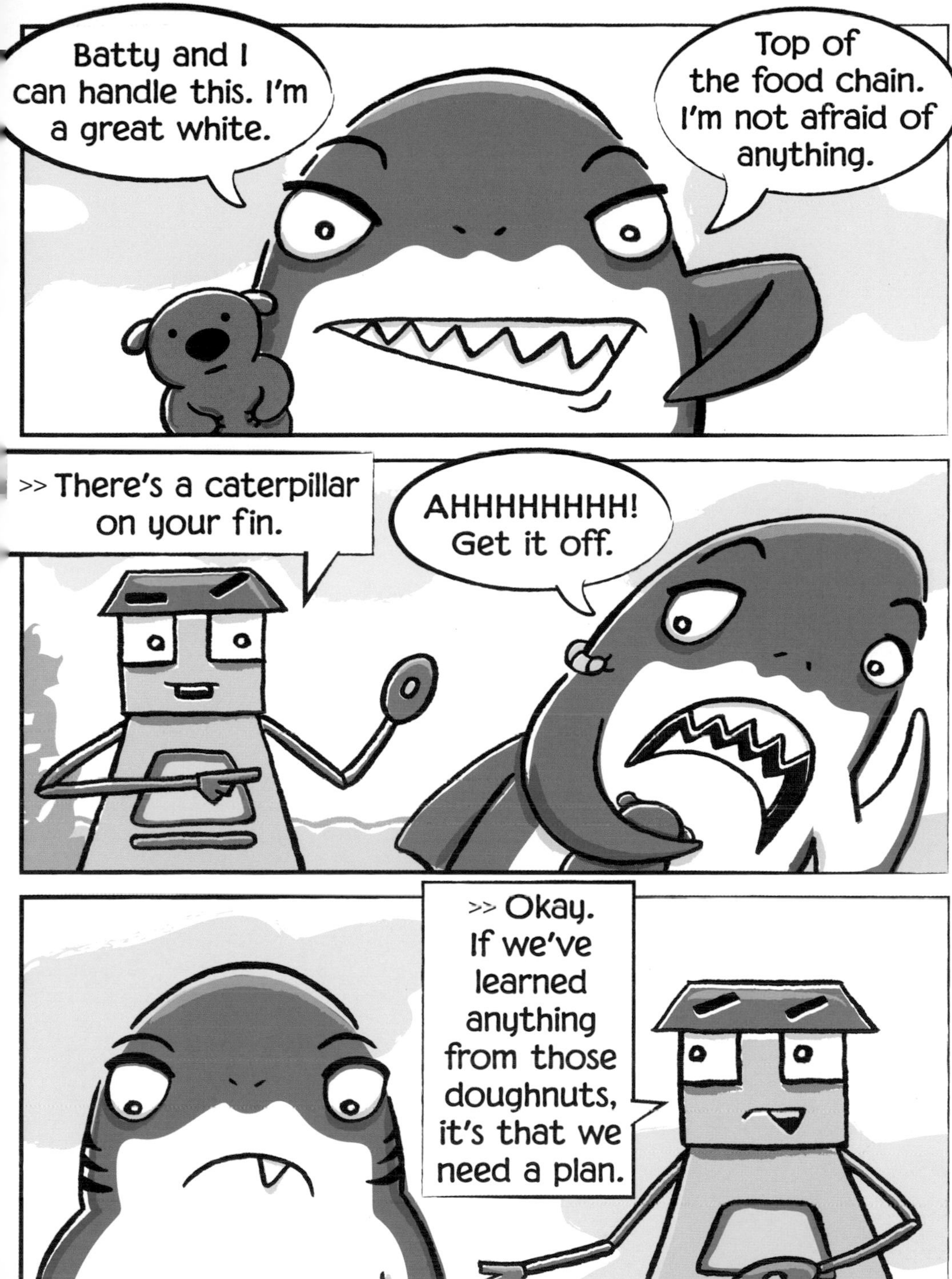
Batty and I can handle this. I'm a great white.
Top of the food chain. I'm not afraid of anything.
>> There's a caterpillar on your fin.
AHHHHHHHH! Get it off.
>> Okay. If we've learned anything from those doughnuts, it's that we need a plan.

HOW TO DEFEAT BULLIES
by BOT

1. ~~Fight them.~~

****

2. ~~Ask them nicely.~~

****

3. Confuse them with a really hard math problem
   until their brains explode.

****

4. Train a squad of baby bodyguards*.
(*NOTE: May take 6-8 months to find enough babies.)

****

5. Open an inter-galactic space portal.
   Push them inside.

****

6. Use a trail of bread crumbs to lead them into
   the forest, where a witch will eat them.
   (Is this the plot of "Hansel and Gretel"???)

****

7. Beat them at their own game.

****

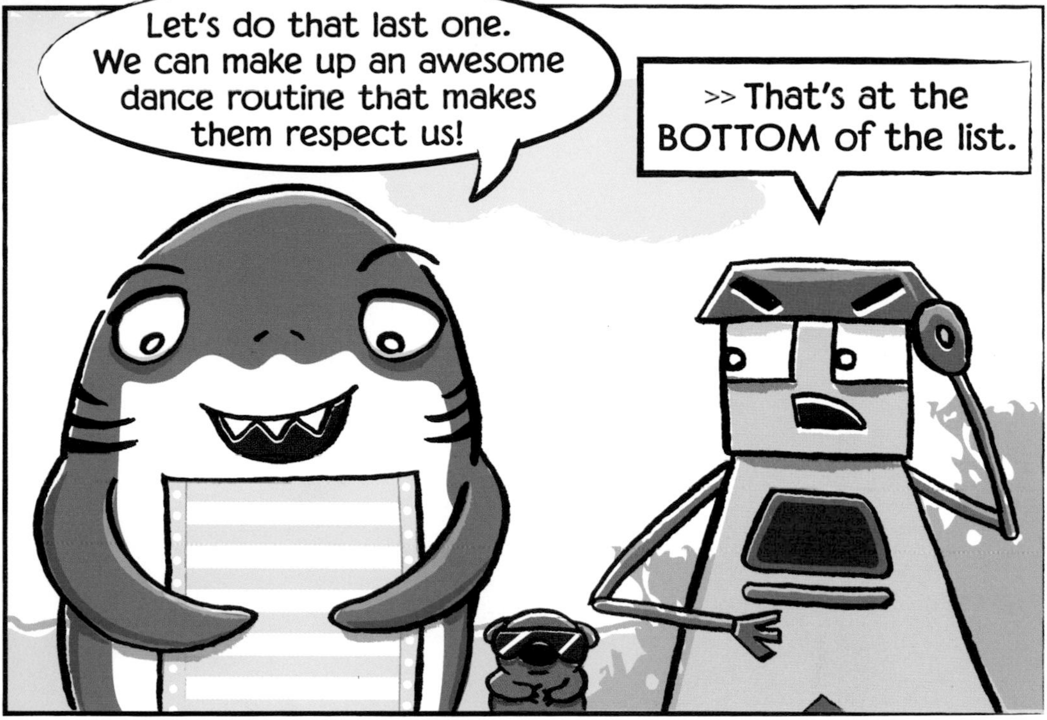
Let's do that last one. We can make up an awesome dance routine that makes them respect us!
>> That's at the BOTTOM of the list.

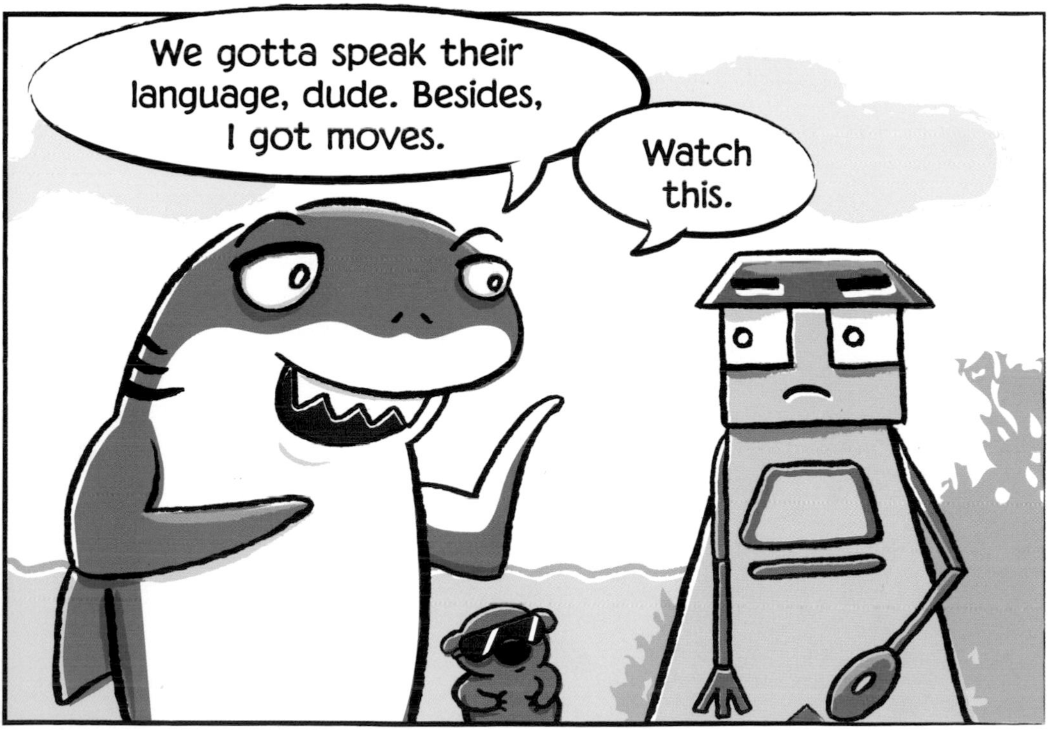
We gotta speak their language, dude. Besides, I got moves.
Watch this.

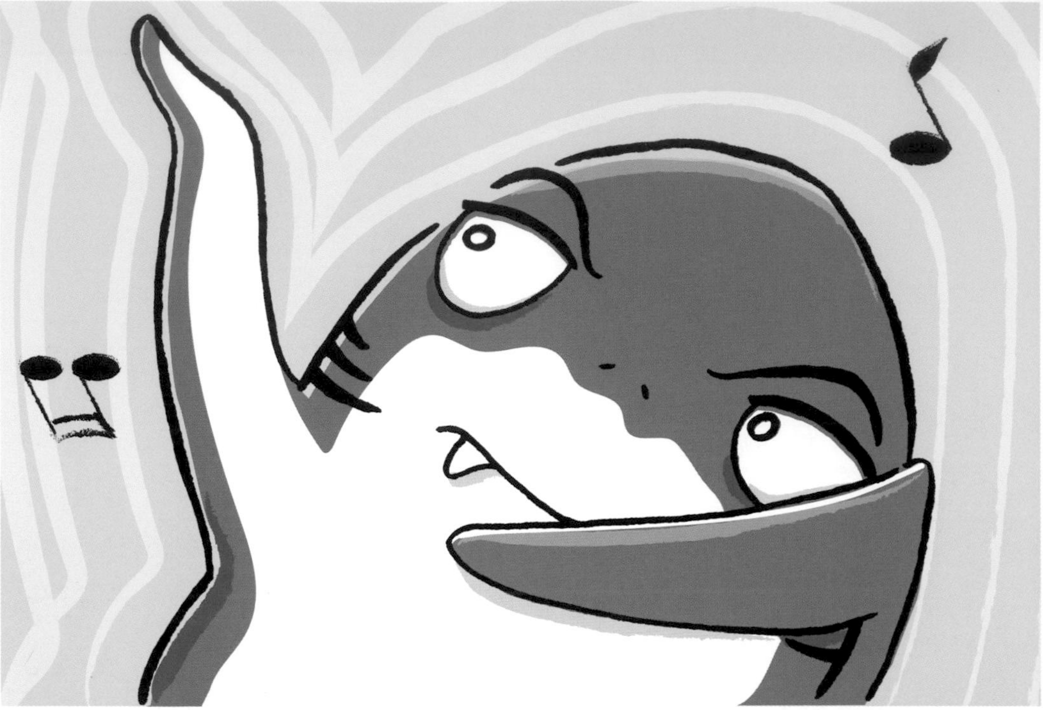

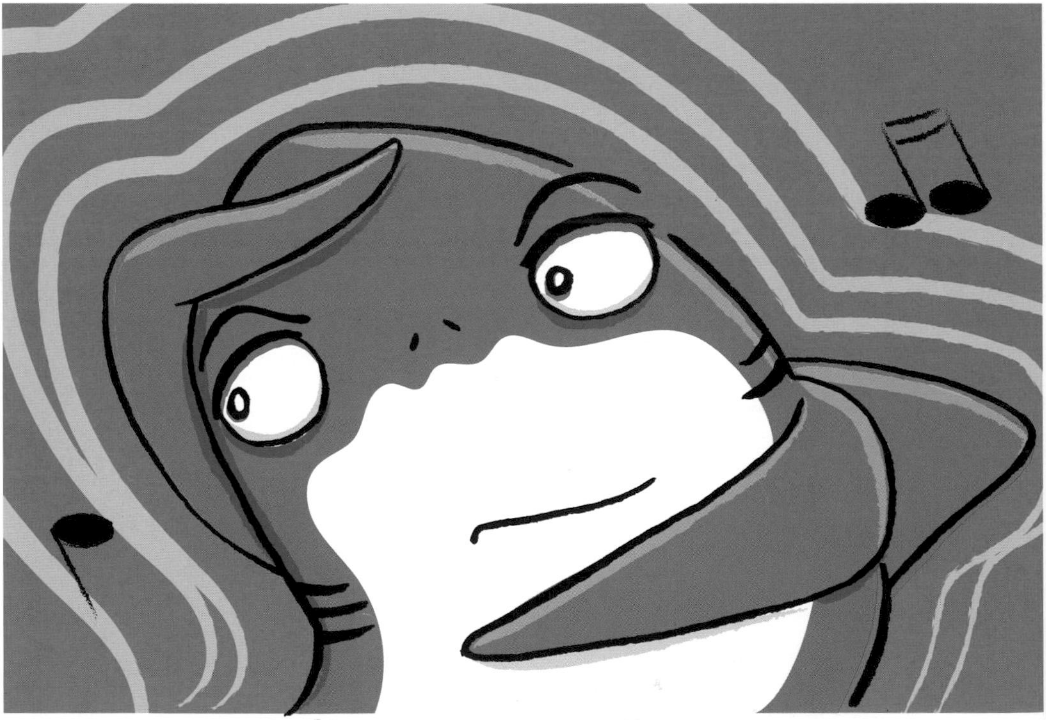

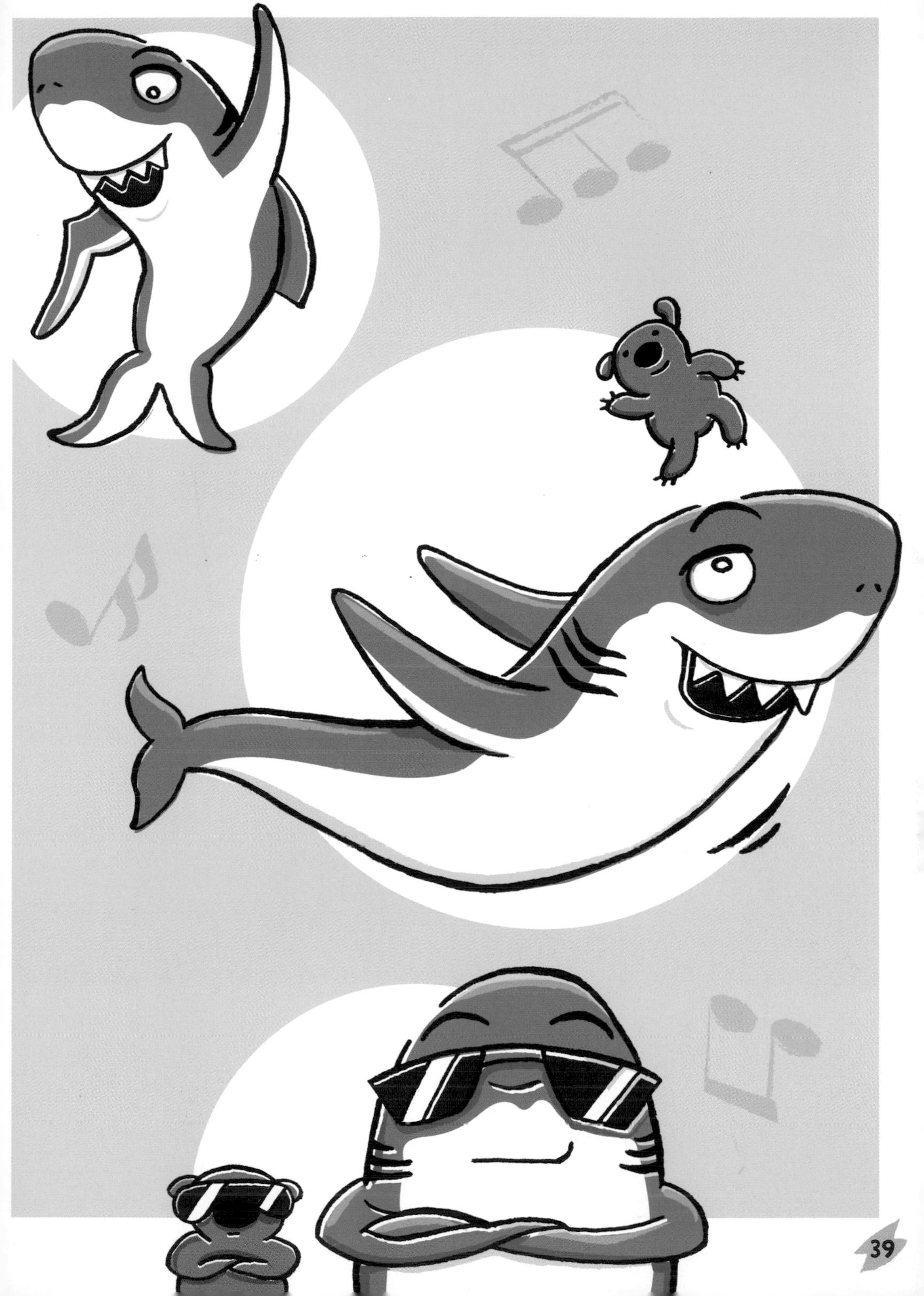

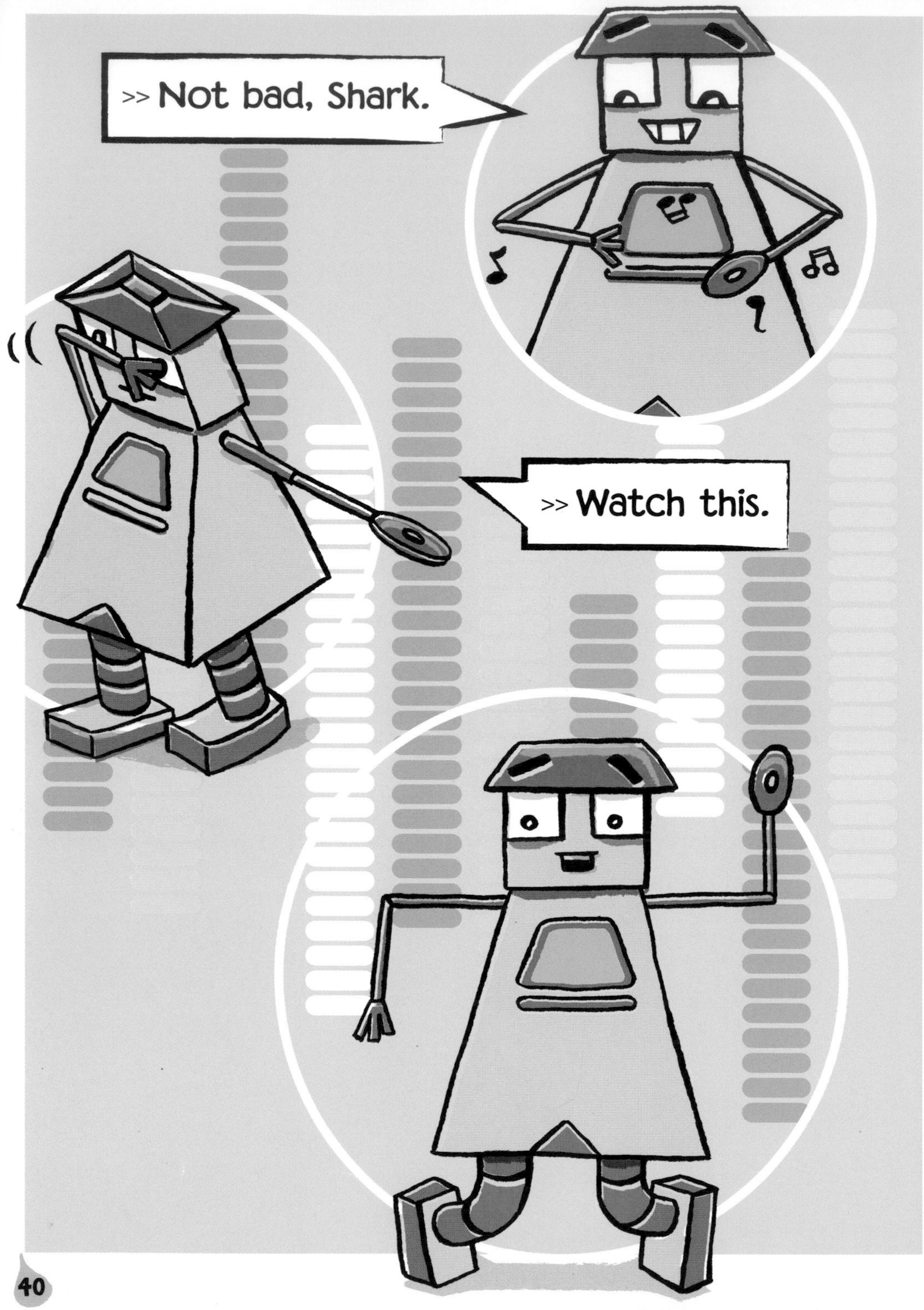
>> Not bad, Shark.
>> Watch this.

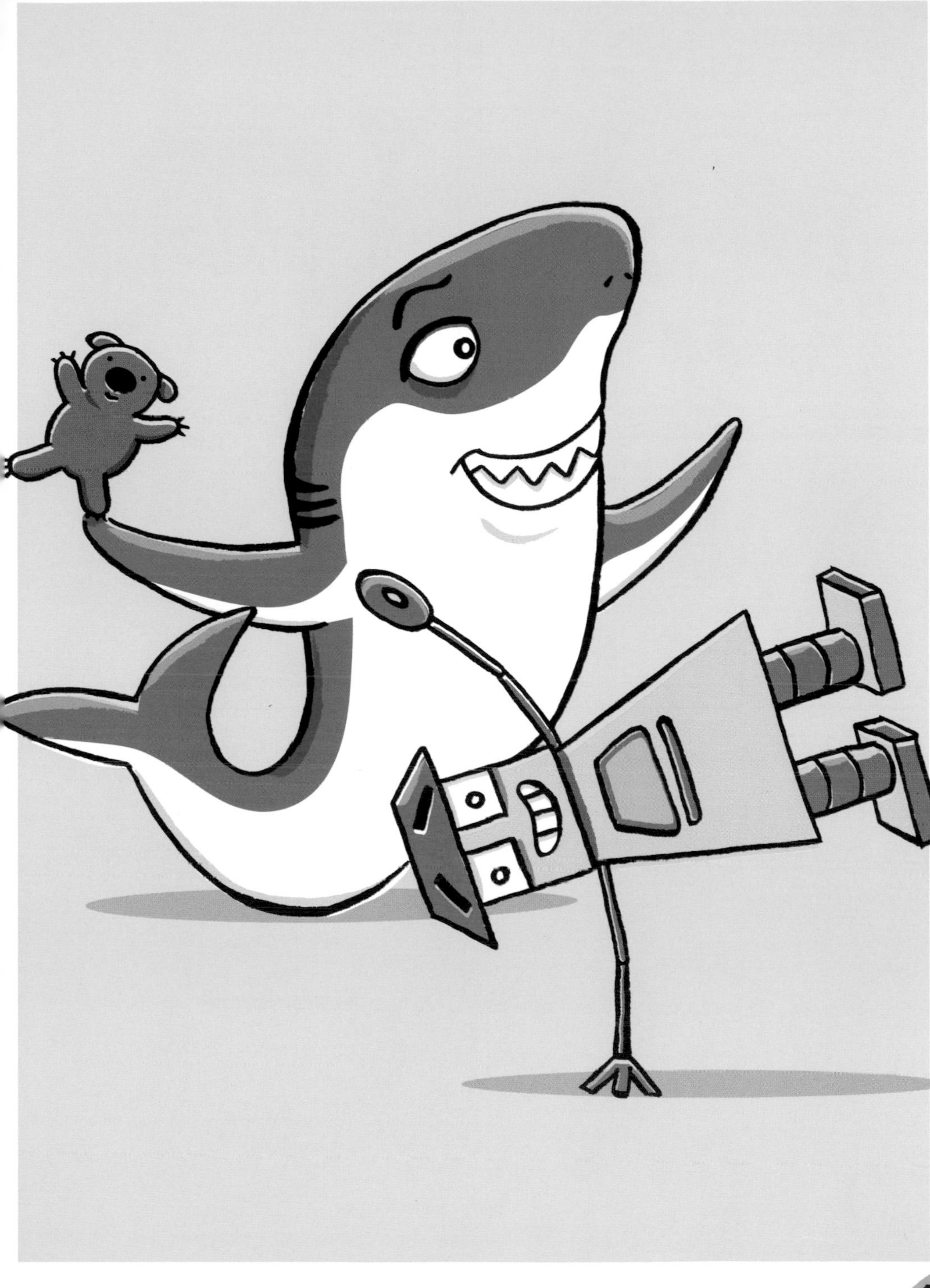

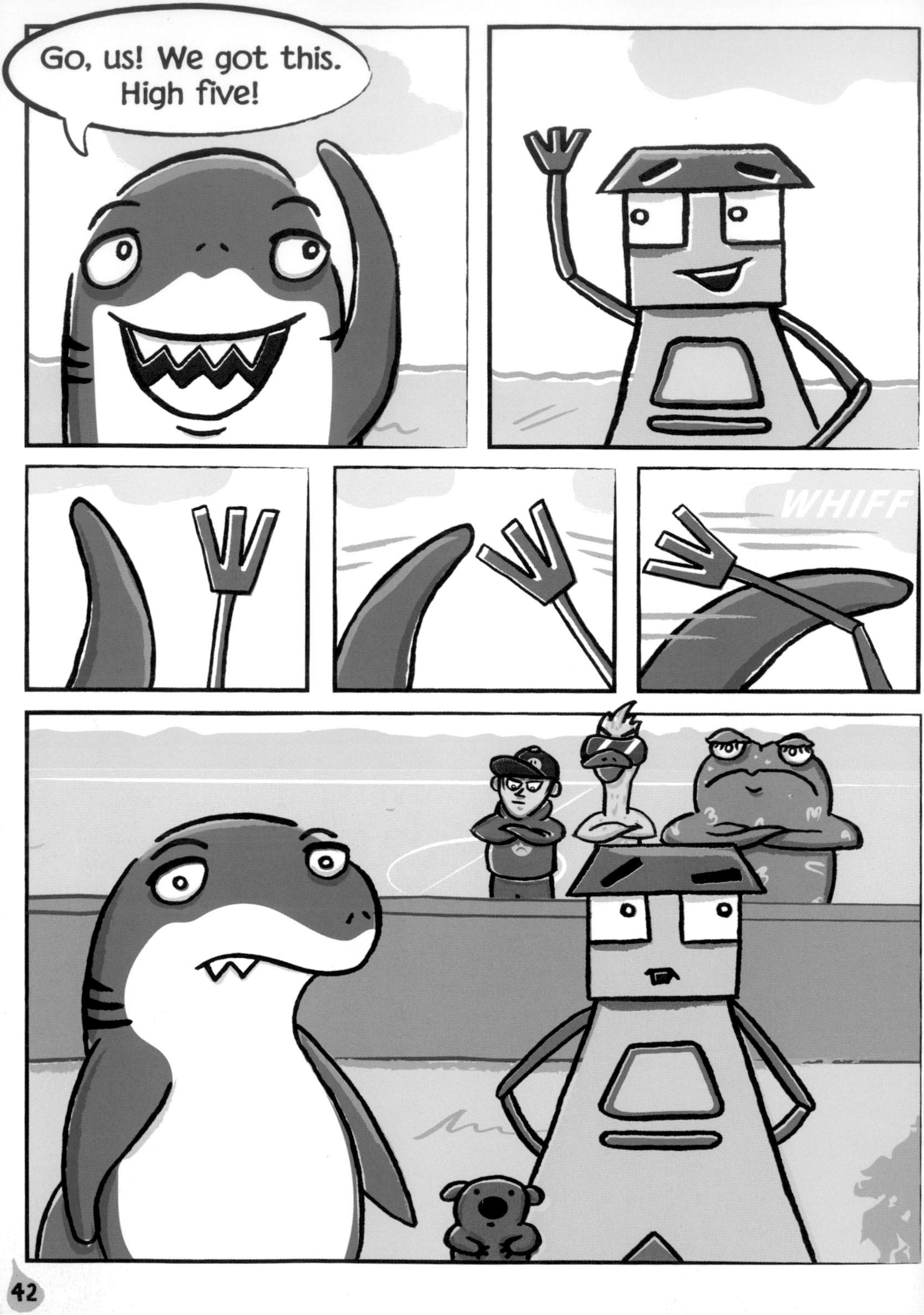
Go, us! We got this.
High five!
WHIFF

Chapter 4

You Call That a Plan?

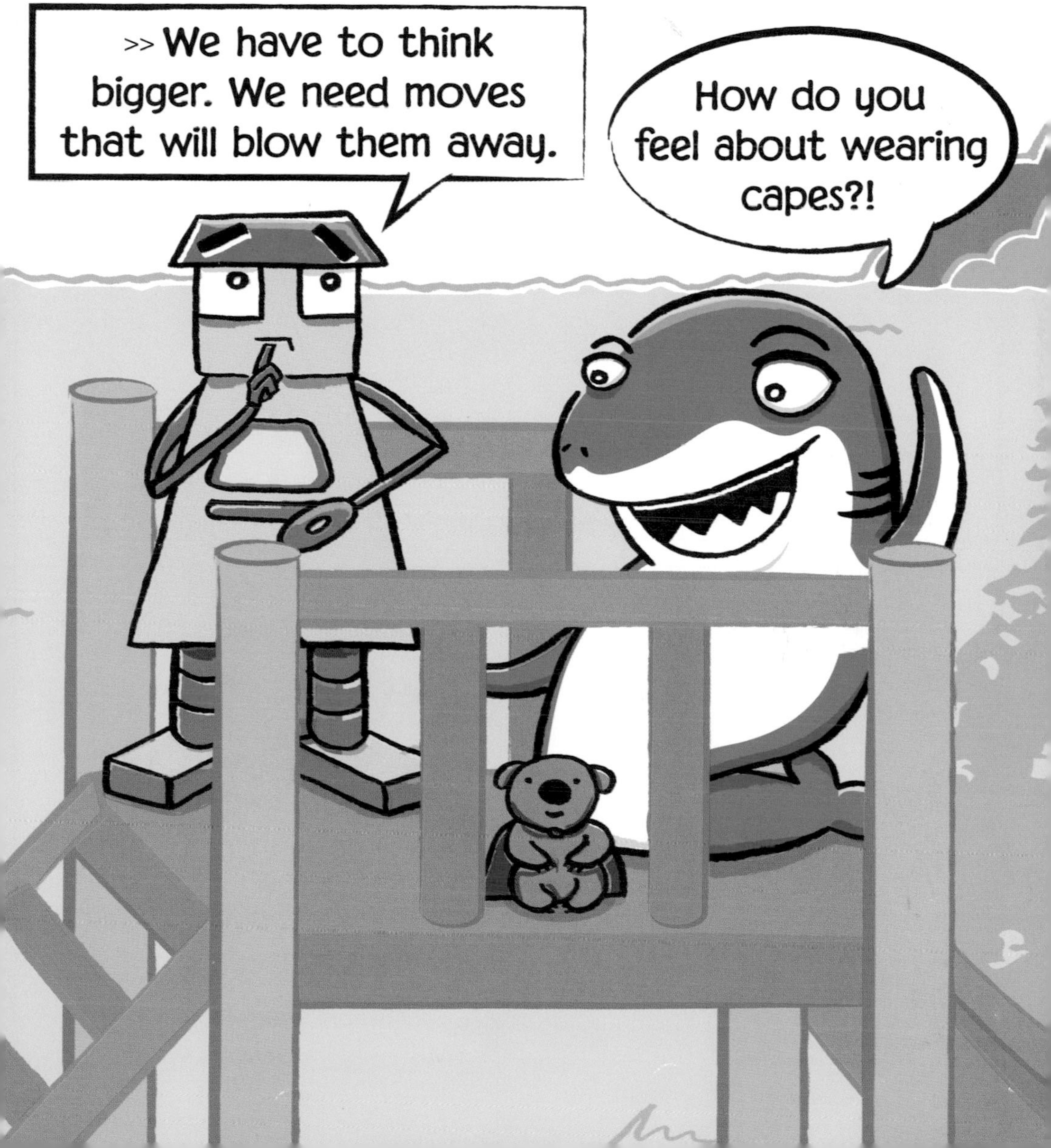

>> We have to think bigger. We need moves that will blow them away.
How do you feel about wearing capes?!

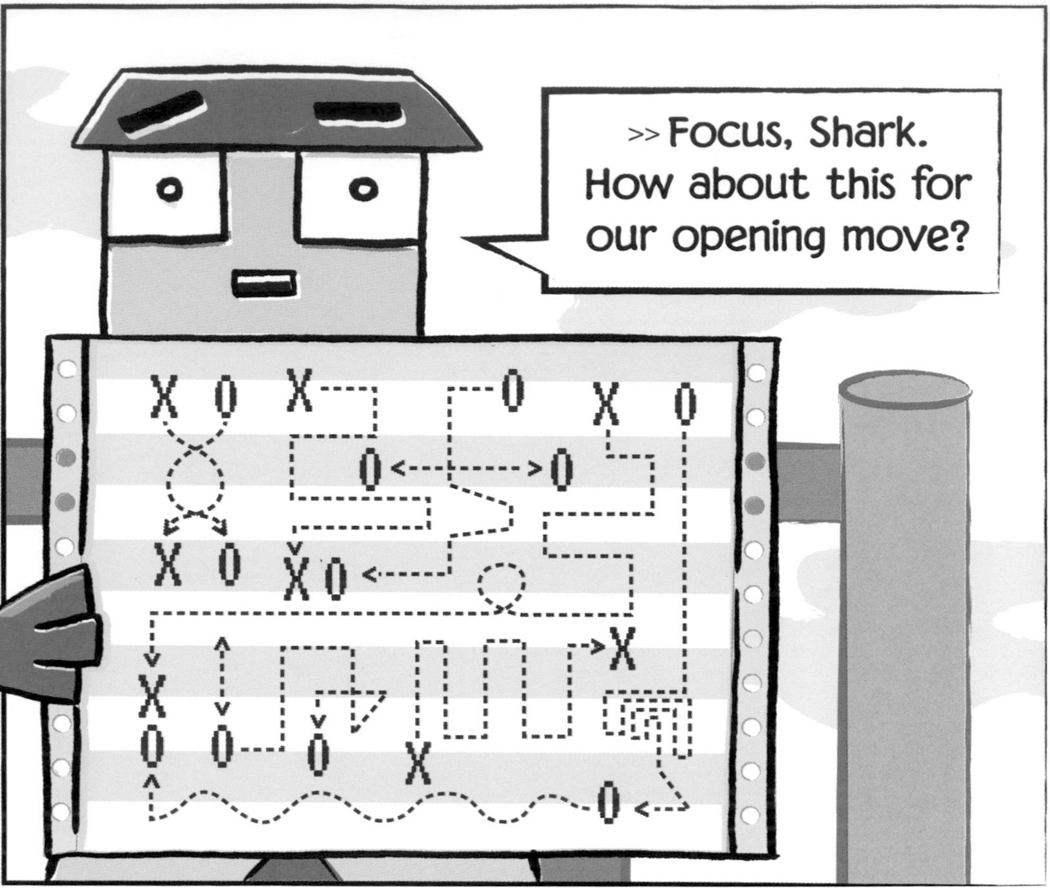
>> Focus, Shark. How about this for our opening move?

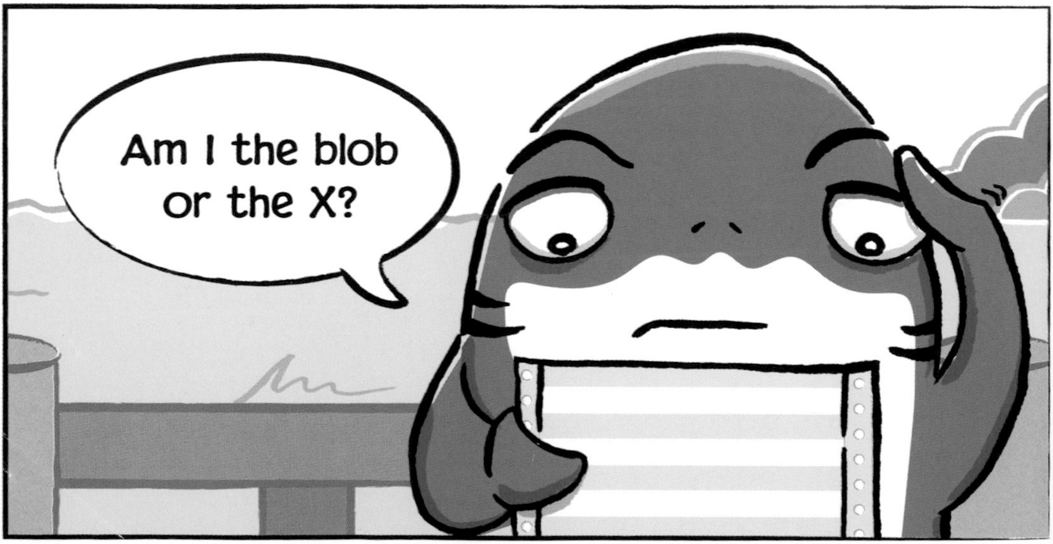
Am I the blob or the X?

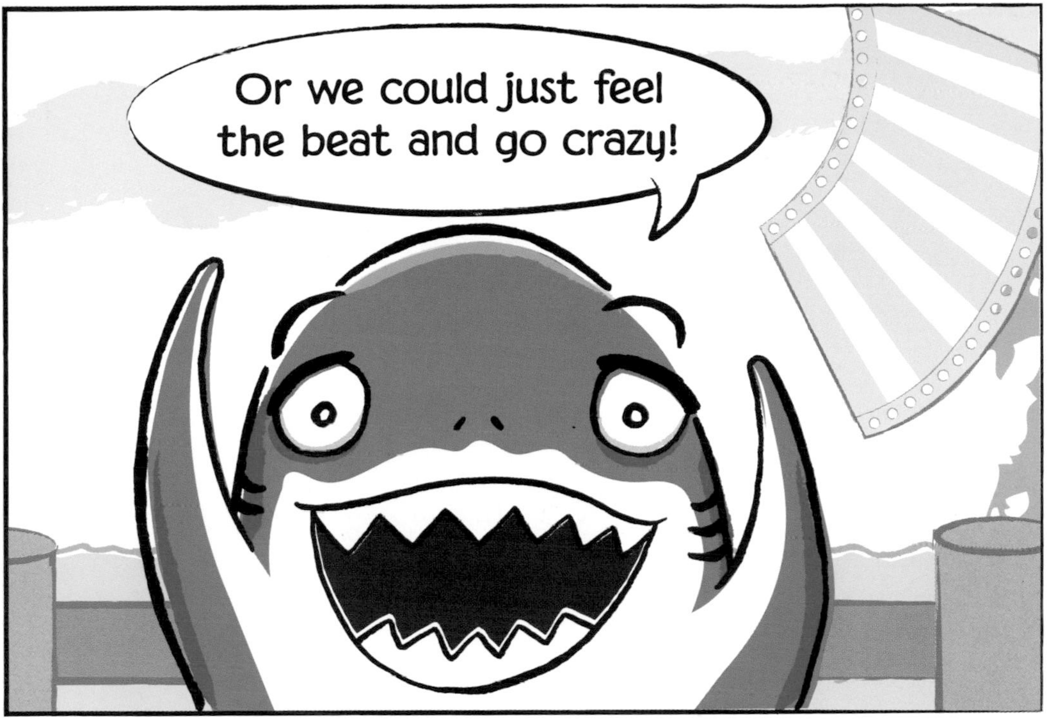
Or we could just feel the beat and go crazy!

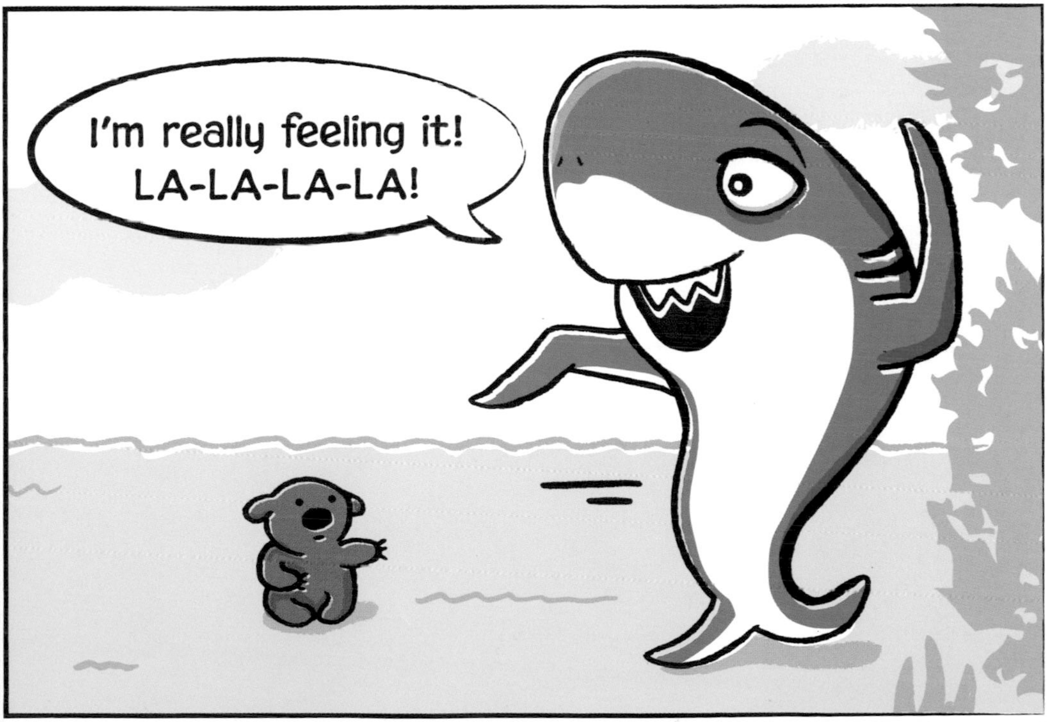
I'm really feeling it! LA-LA-LA-LA!

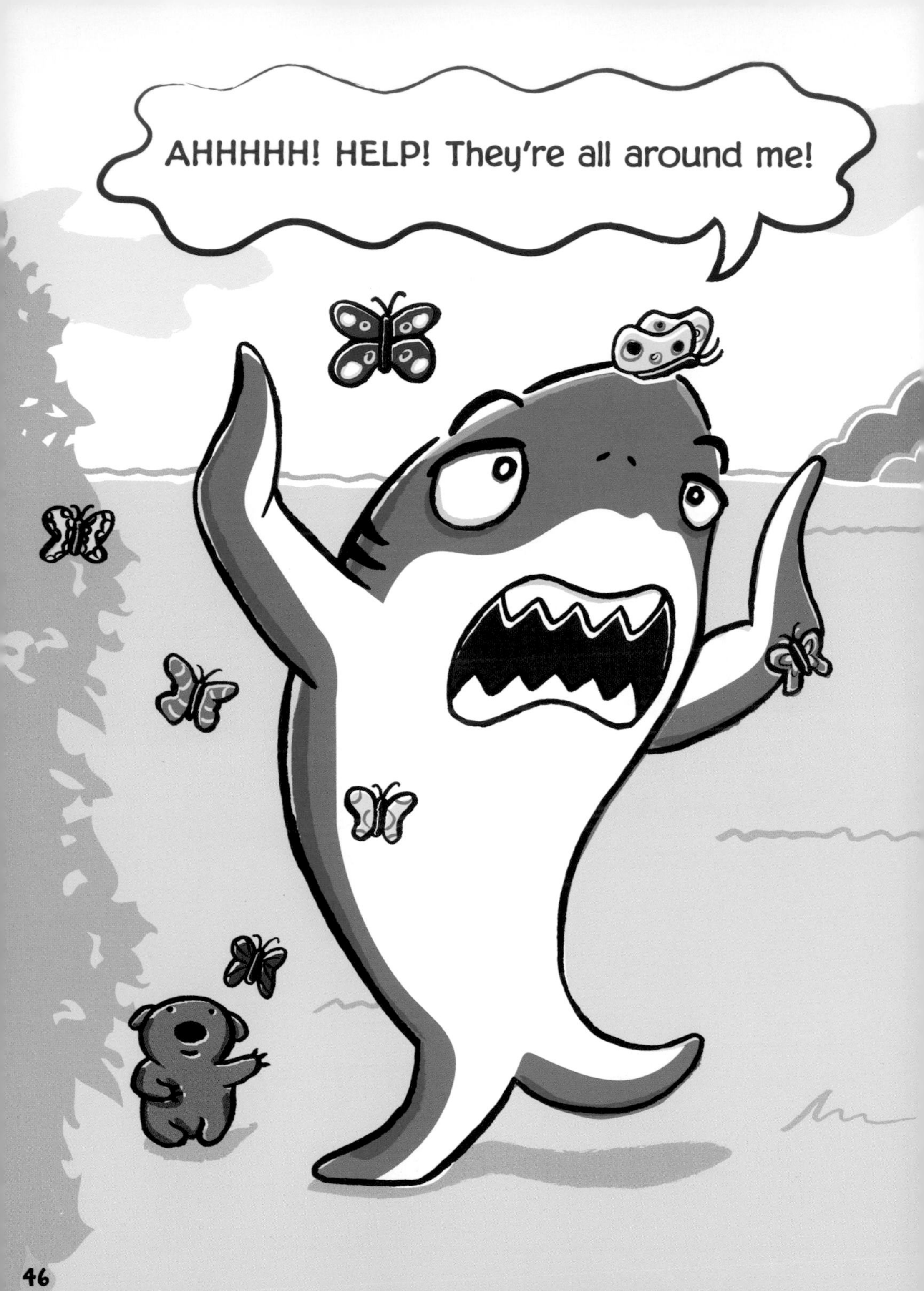
AHHHHH! HELP! They're all around me!

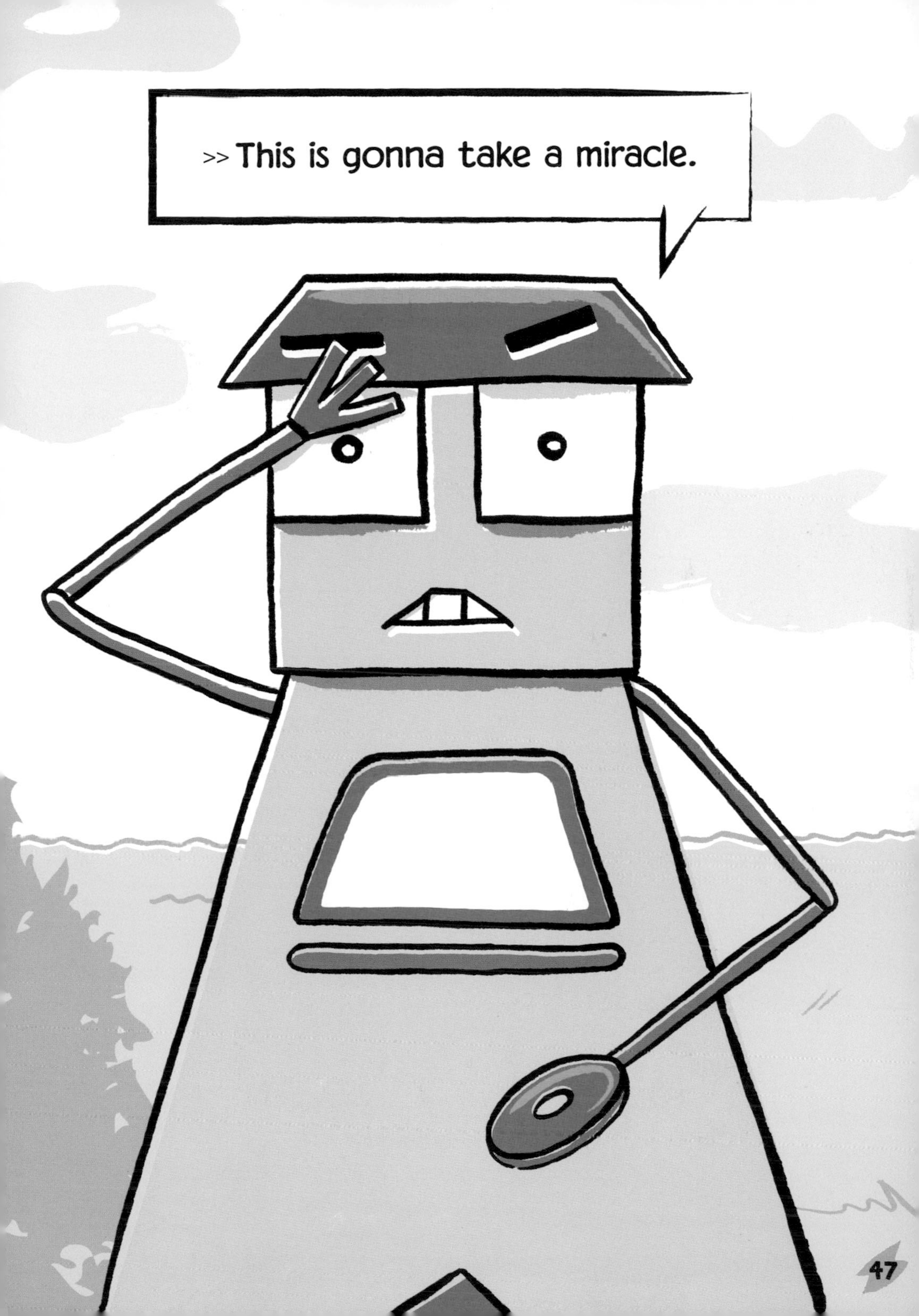
>> This is gonna take a miracle.

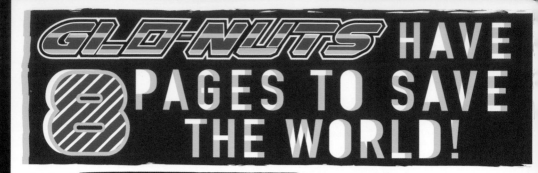

GLO-NUTS HAVE 8 PAGES TO SAVE THE WORLD!

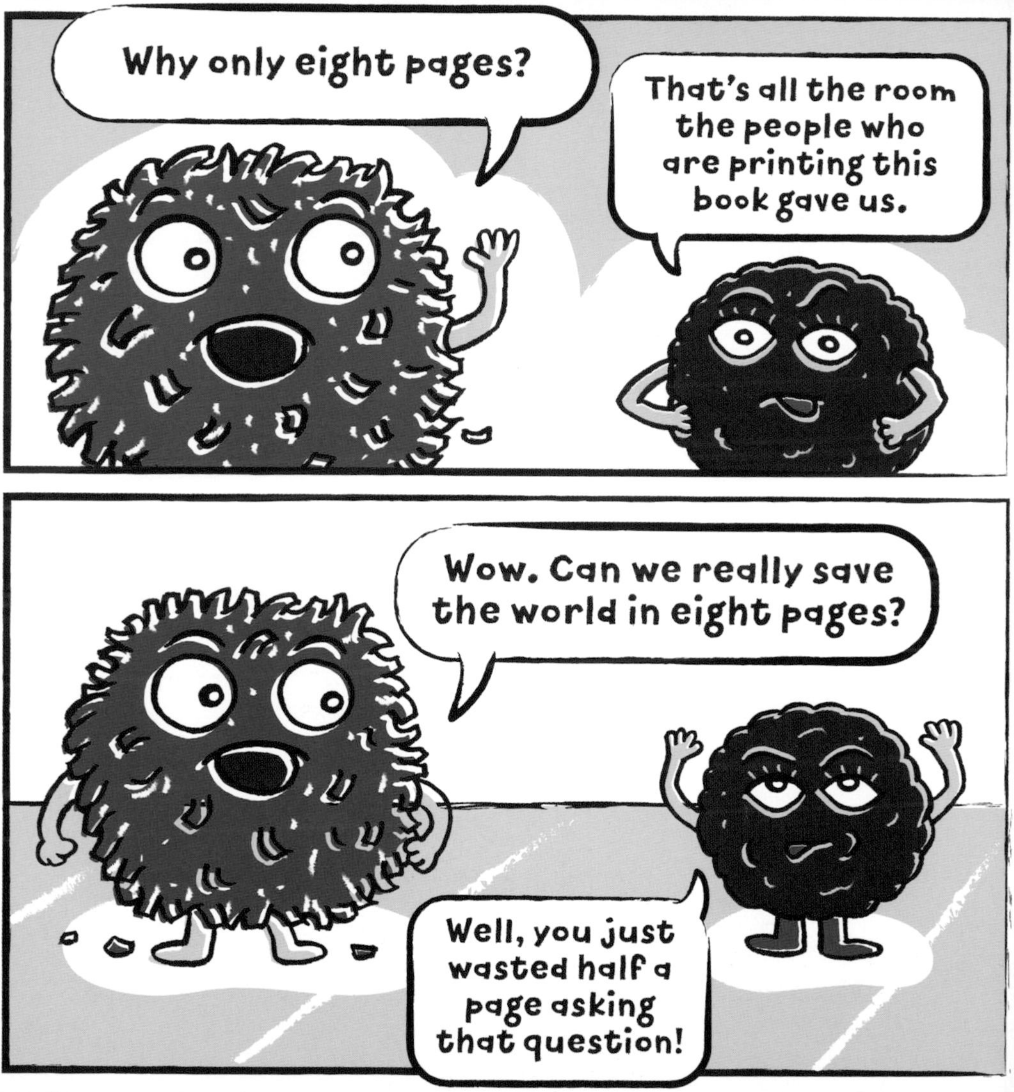
Why only eight pages?
That's all the room the people who are printing this book gave us.
Wow. Can we really save the world in eight pages?
Well, you just wasted half a page asking that question!

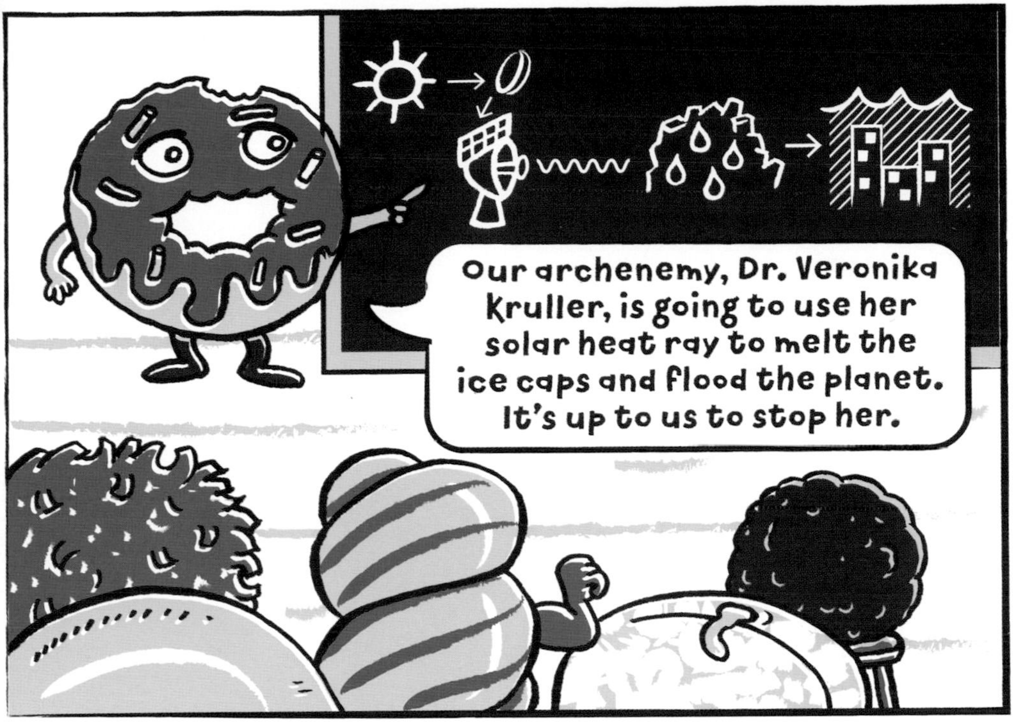
Our archenemy, Dr. Veronika Kruller, is going to use her solar heat ray to melt the ice caps and flood the planet. It's up to us to stop her.

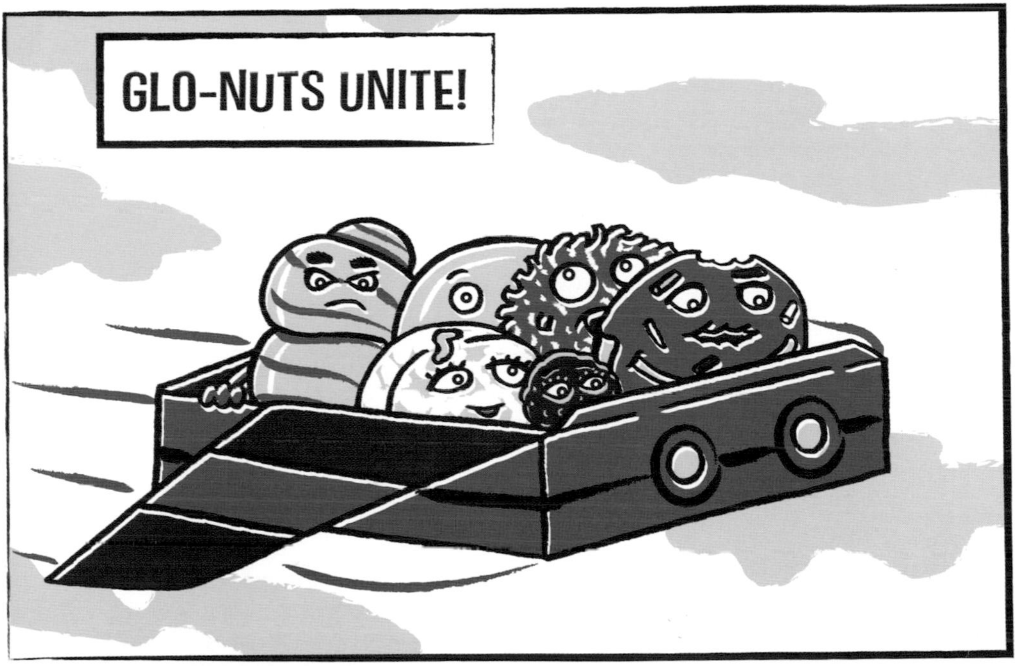
GLO-NUTS UNITE!

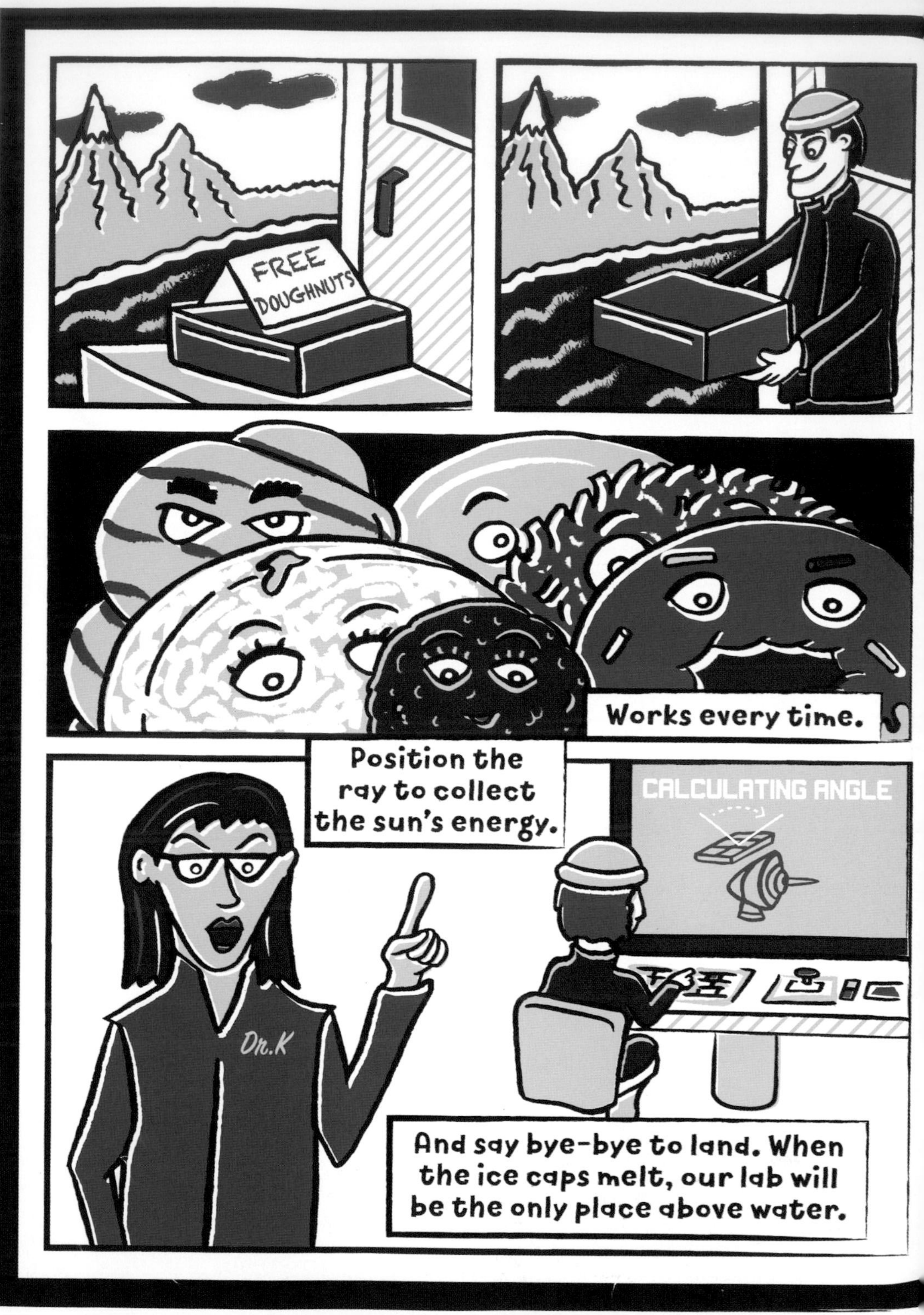
FREE DOUGHNUTS
Works every time.
Position the ray to collect the sun's energy.
CALCULATING ANGLE
Dr.K
And say bye-bye to land. When the ice caps melt, our lab will be the only place above water.

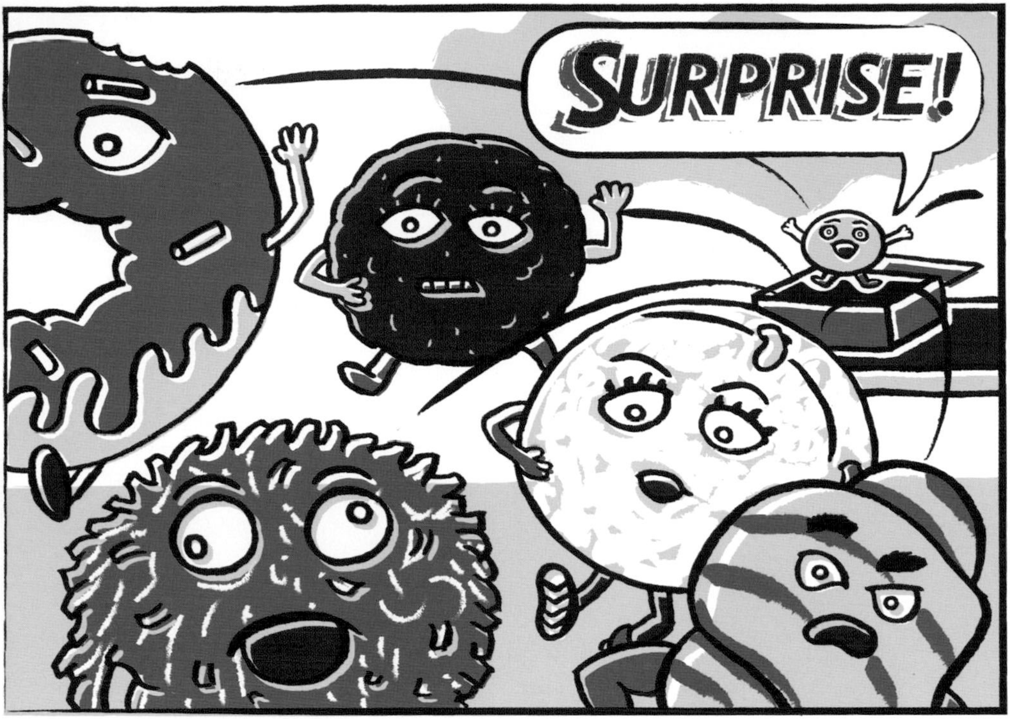
SURPRISE!

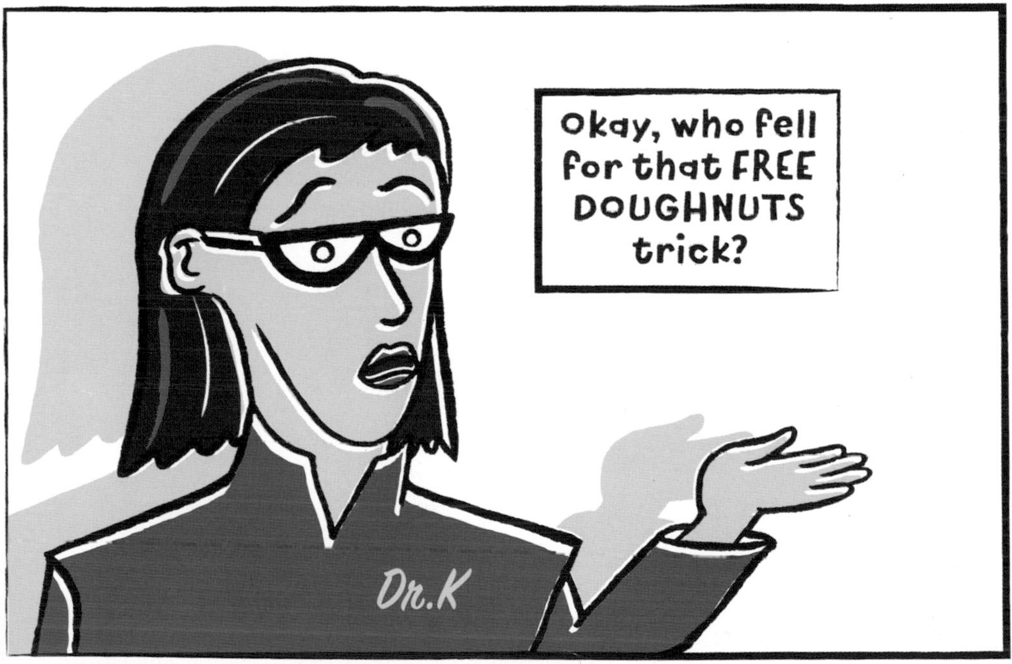
Okay, who fell for that FREE DOUGHNUTS trick?
Dr.K

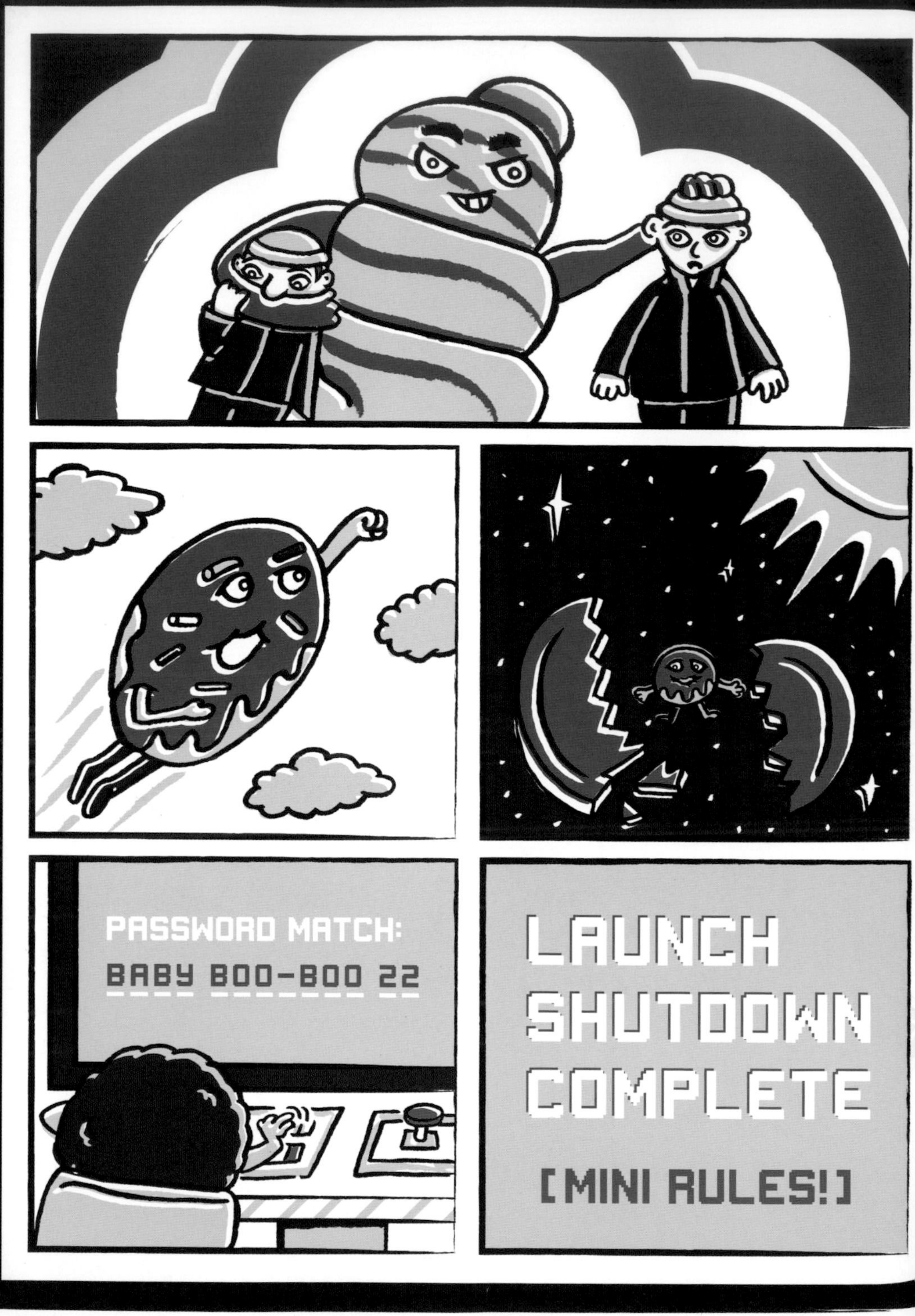
PASSWORD MATCH:
BABY BOO-BOO 22
LAUNCH SHUTDOWN COMPLETE
[MINI RULES!]

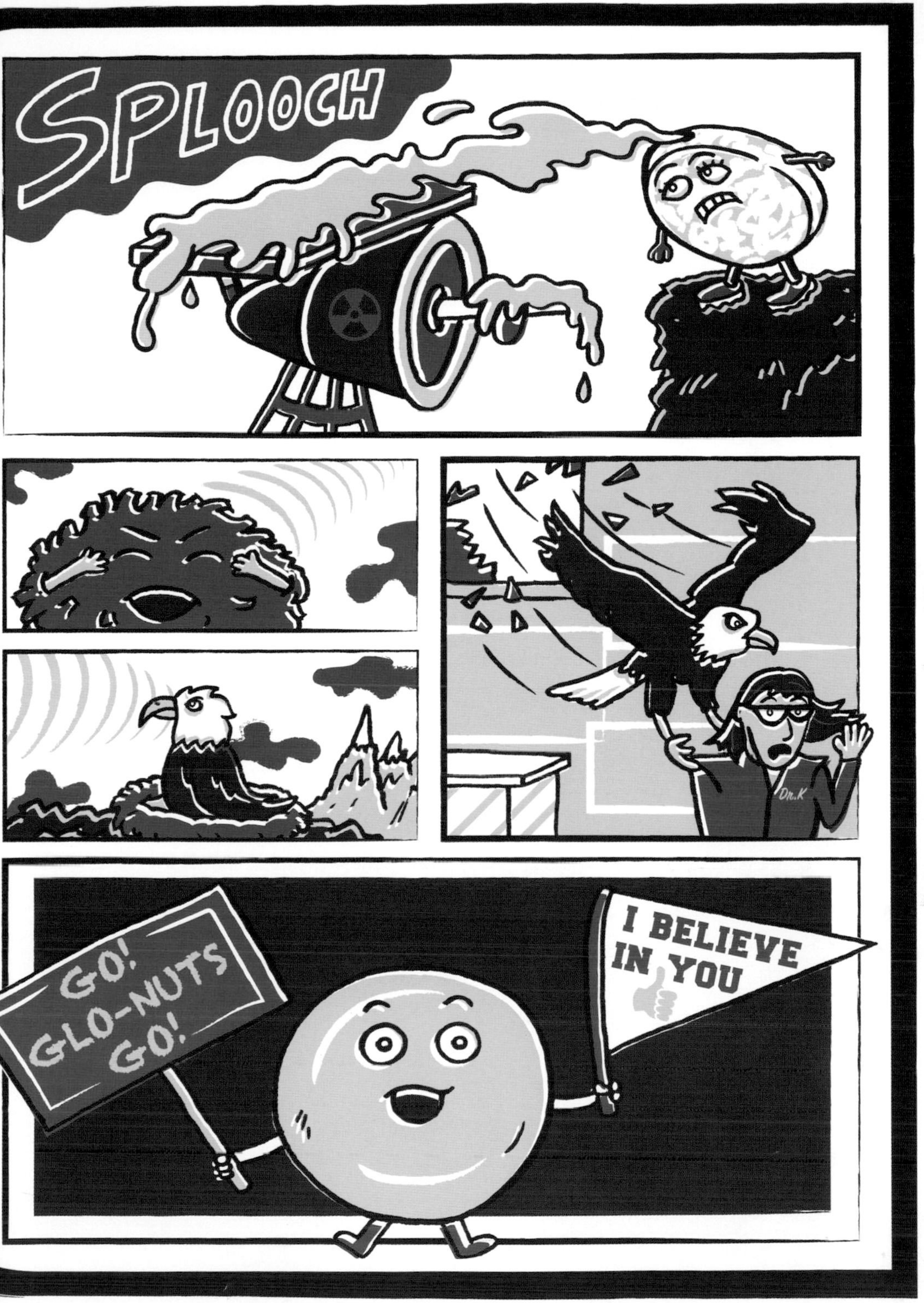
SPLOOCH
Dr. K
GO! GLO-NUTS GO!
I BELIEVE IN YOU

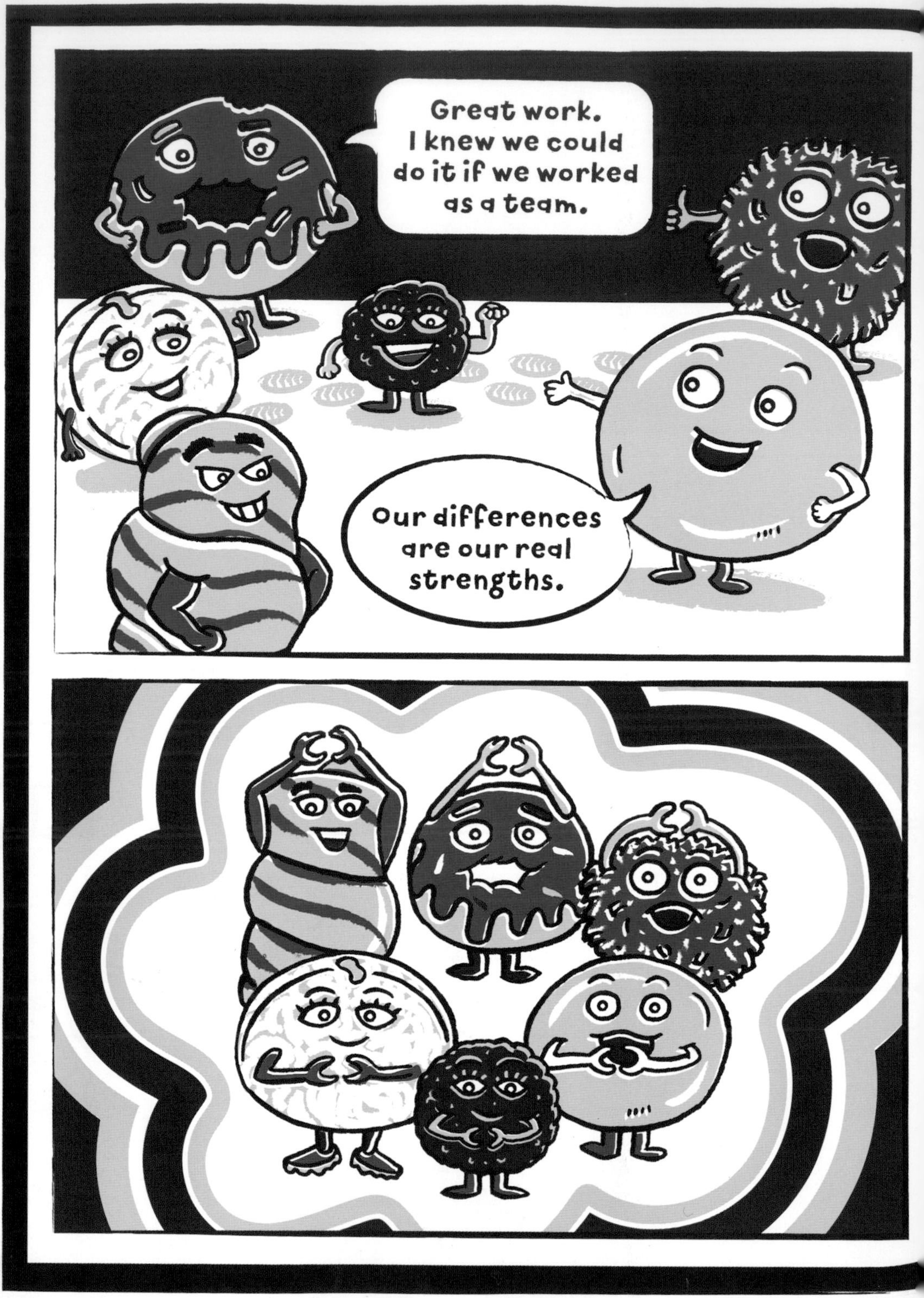
Great work. I knew we could do it if we worked as a team.
Our differences are our real strengths.

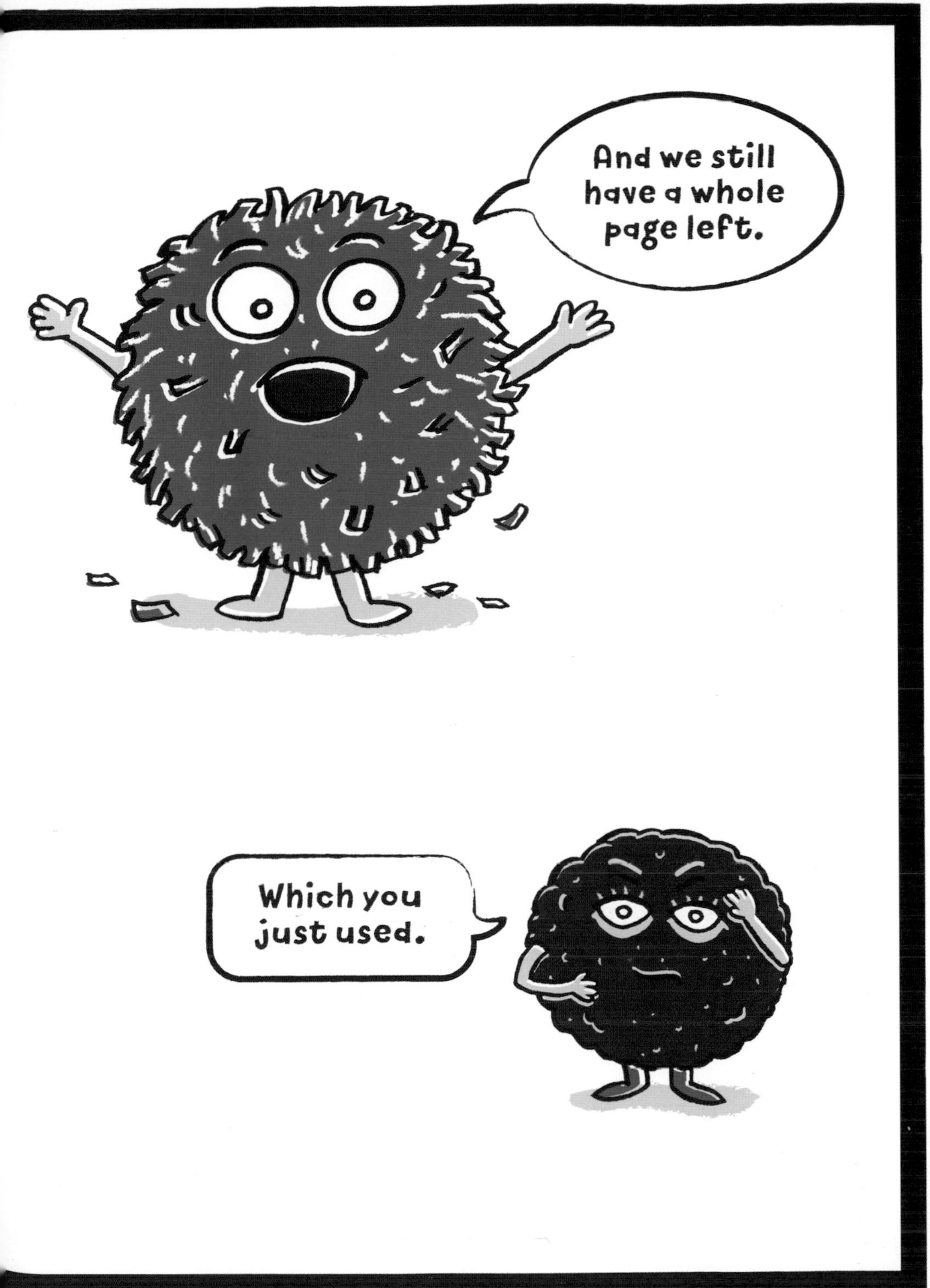
And we still have a whole page left.
Which you just used.

Chapter 5

The Challenge

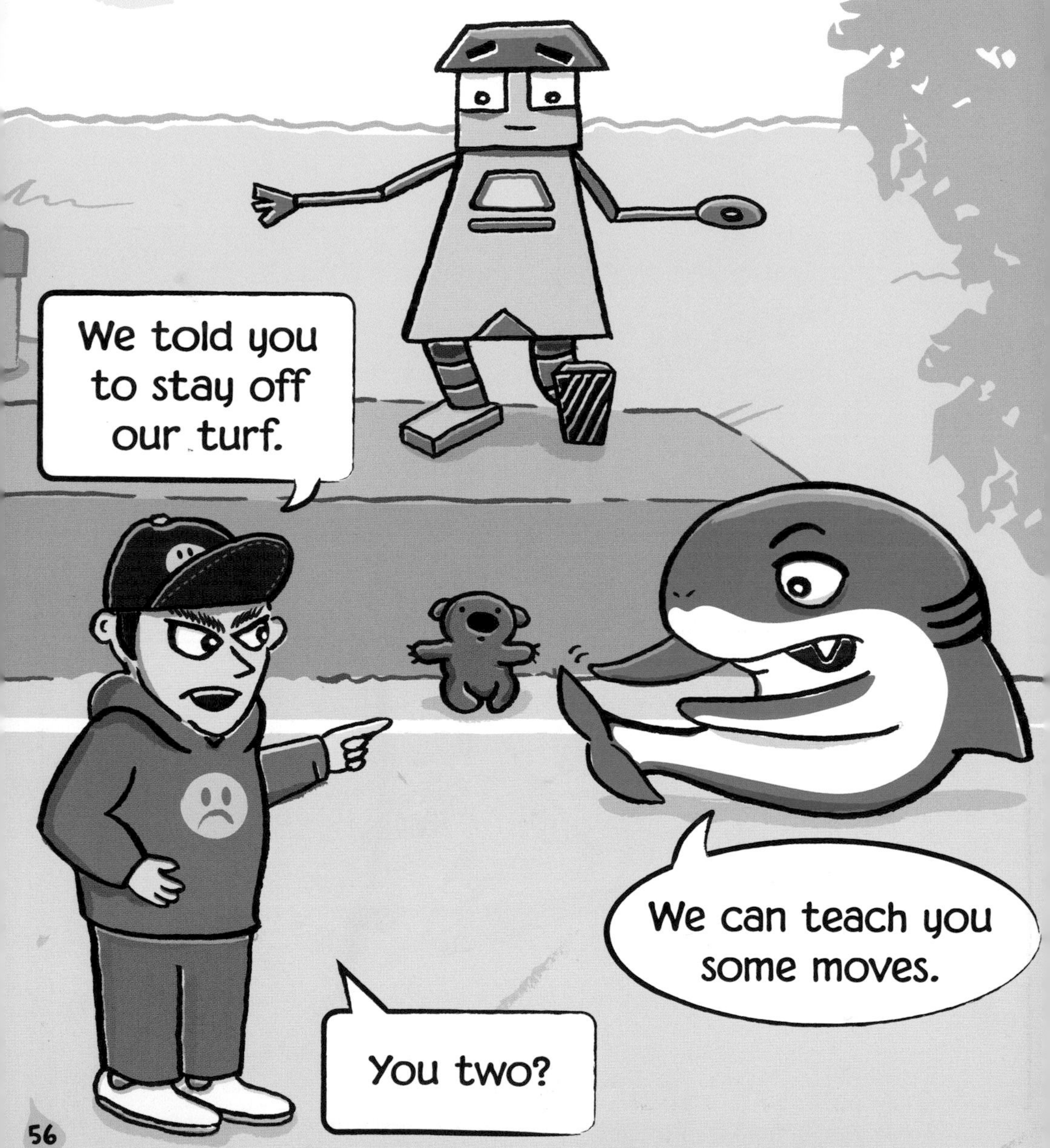
We told you to stay off our turf.
We can teach you some moves.
You two?

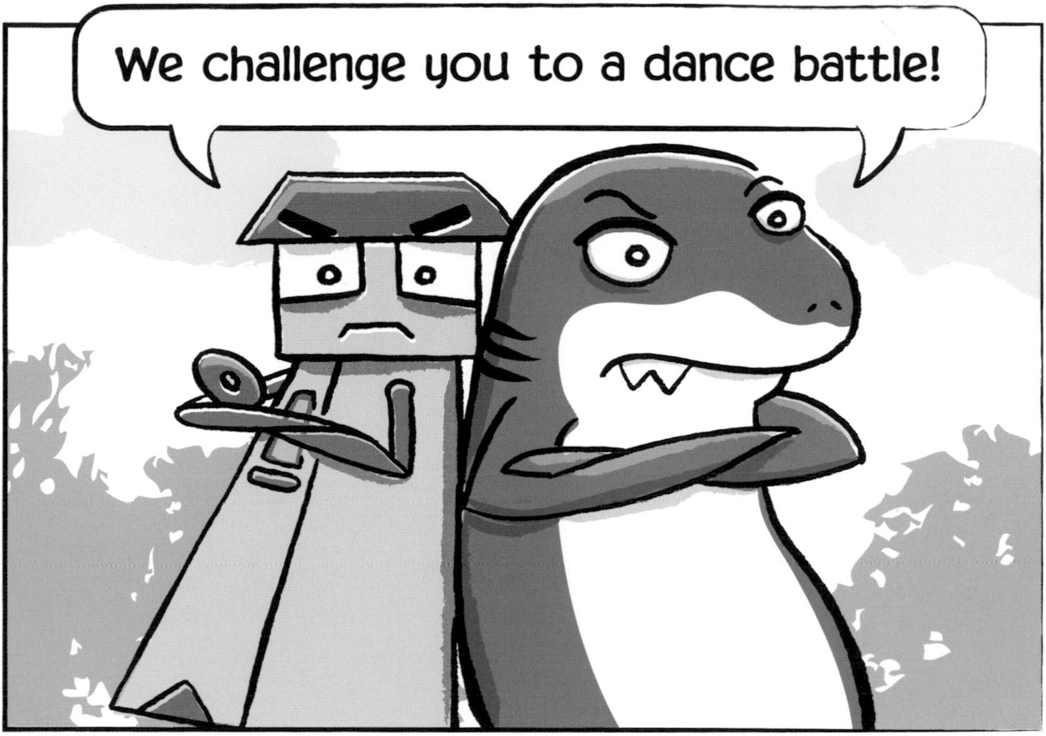
We challenge you to a dance battle!

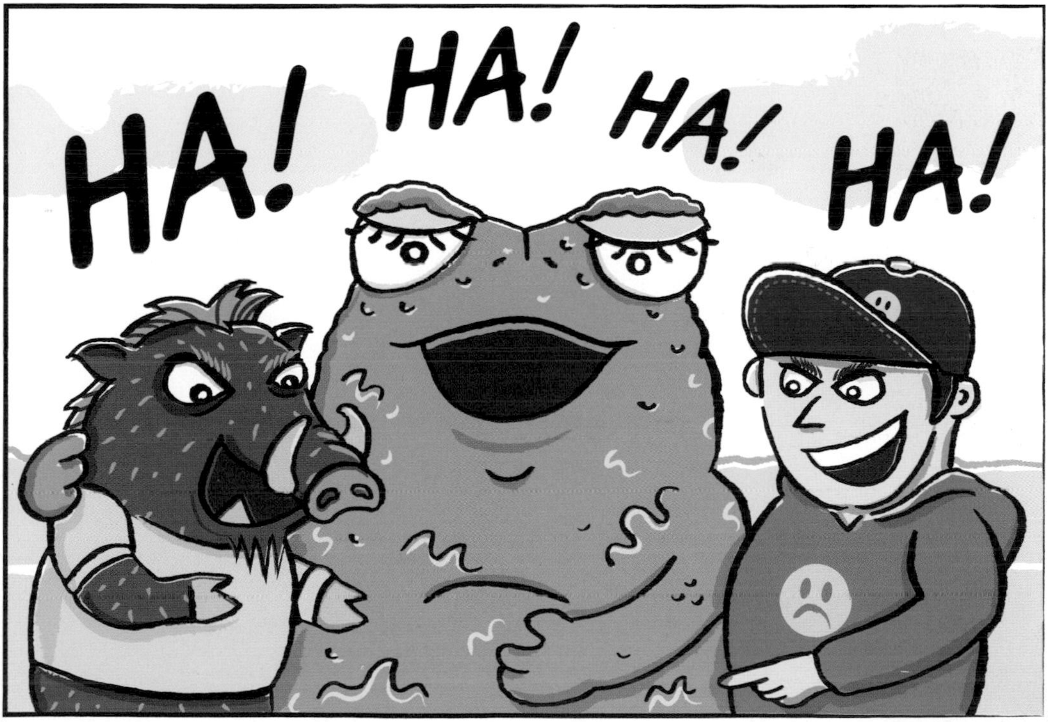
HA!
HA!
HA!
HA!

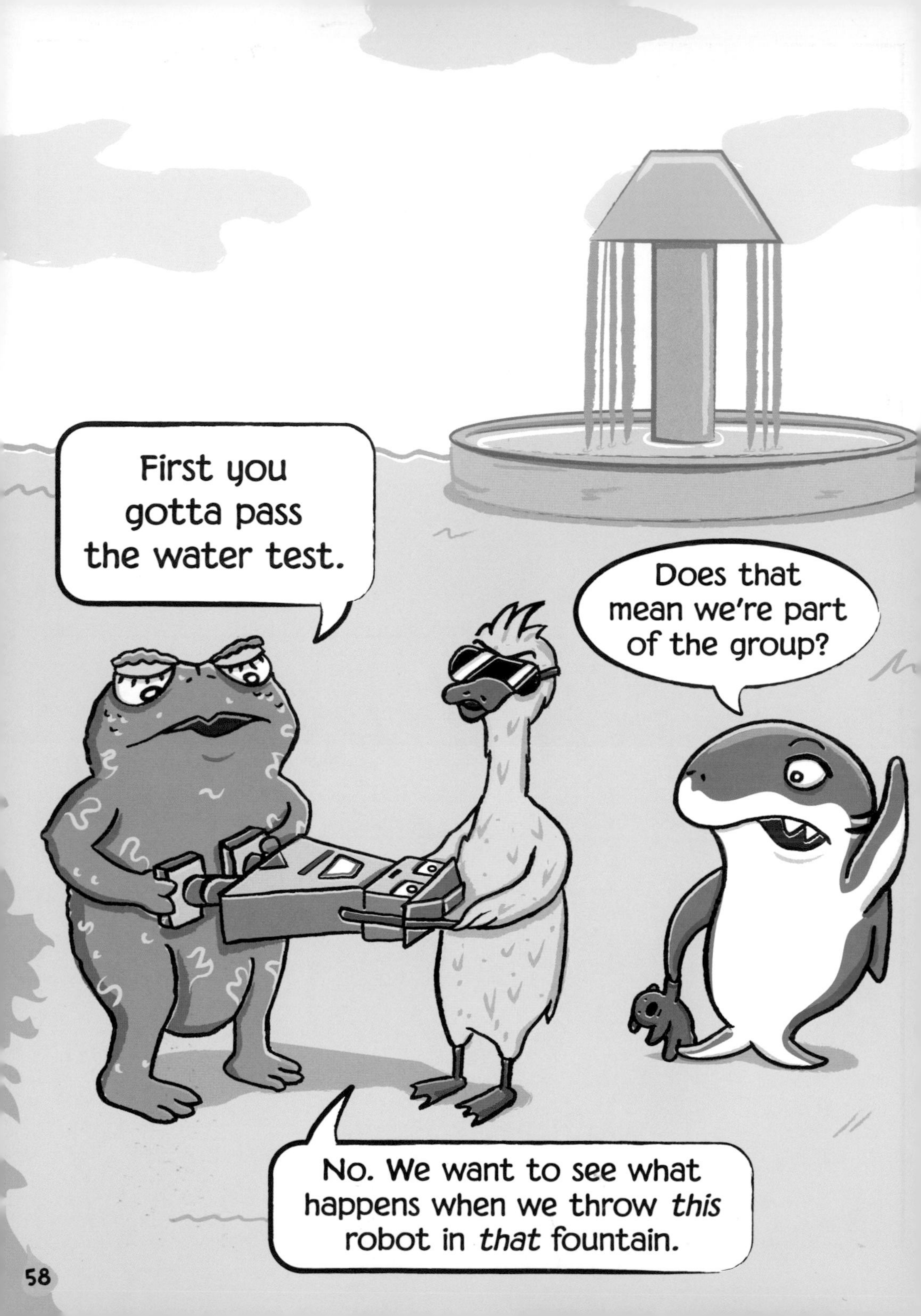
First you gotta pass the water test.
Does that mean we're part of the group?
No. We want to see what happens when we throw *this* robot in *that* fountain.

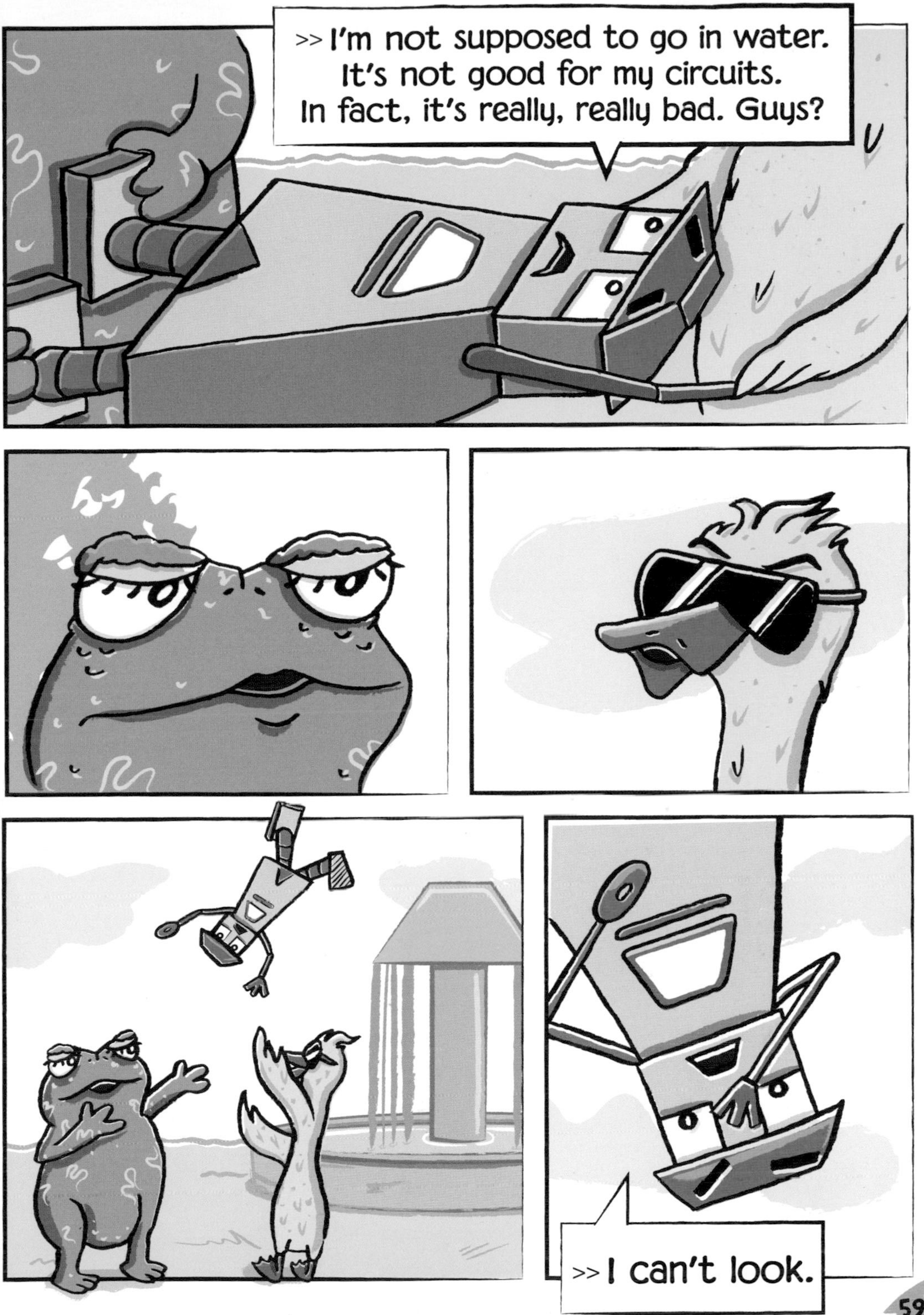
>> I'm not supposed to go in water. It's not good for my circuits. In fact, it's really, really bad. Guys?
>> I can't look.

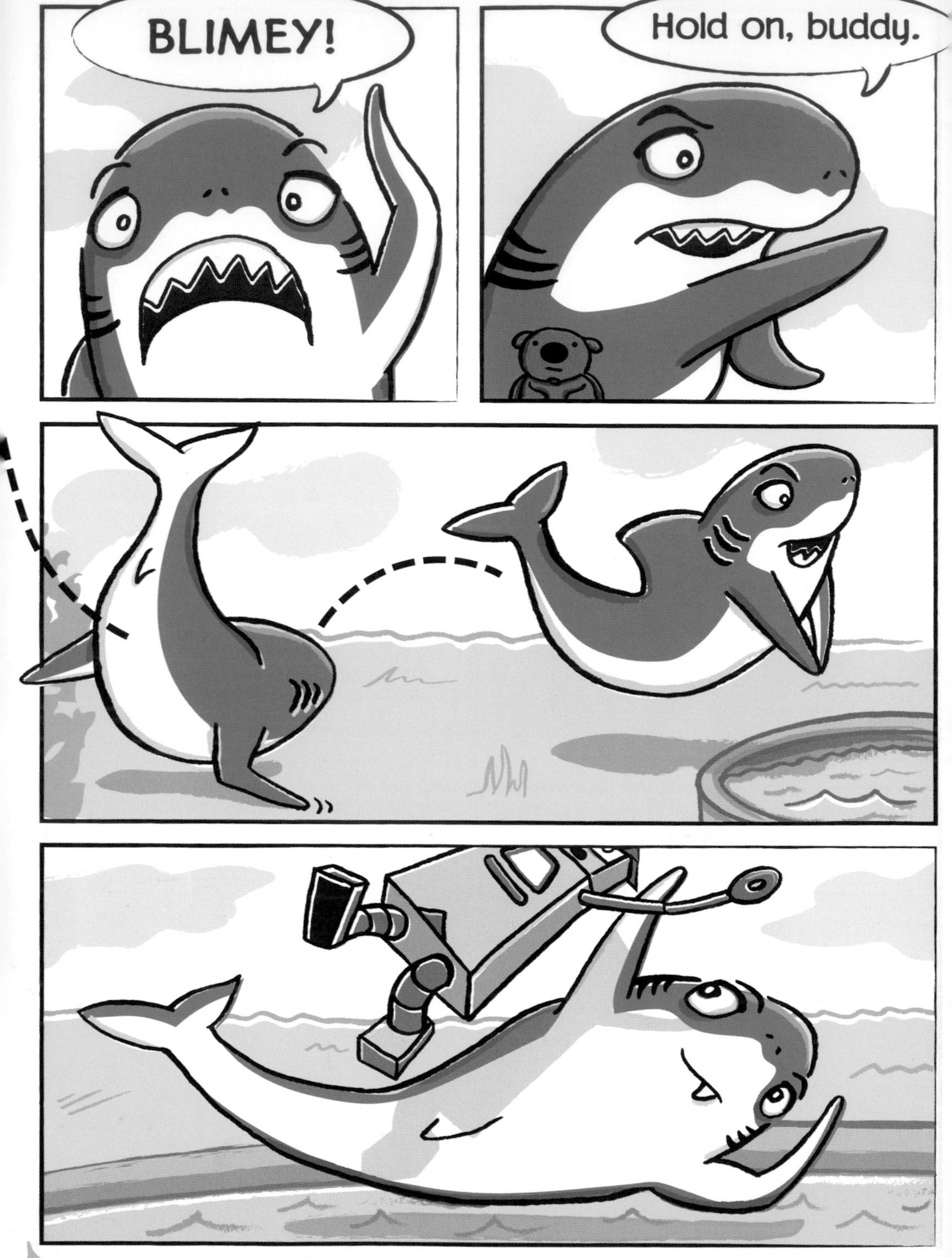
BLIMEY!
Hold on, buddy.

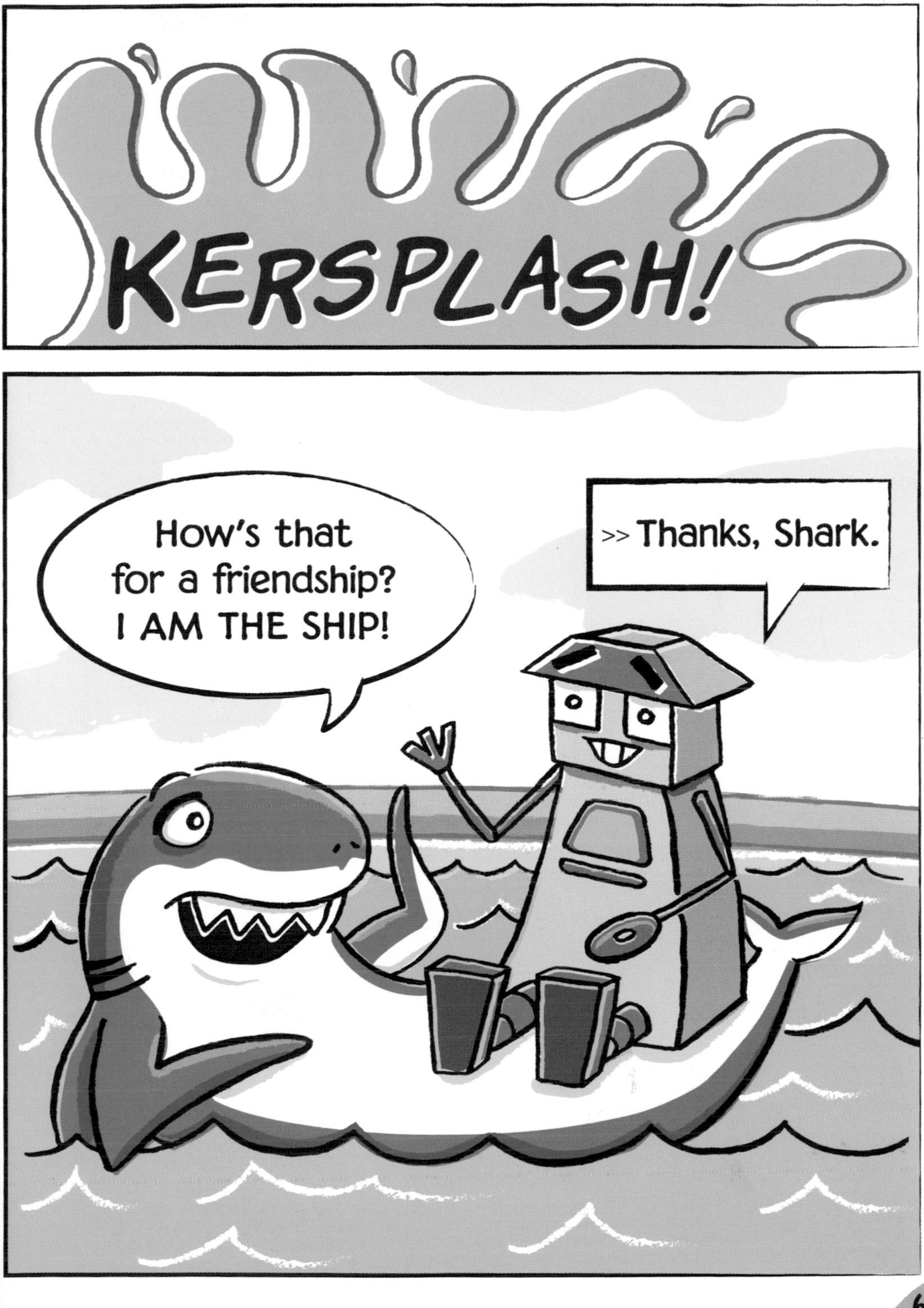
KERSPLASH!
How's that for a friendship? I AM THE SHIP!
>> Thanks, Shark.

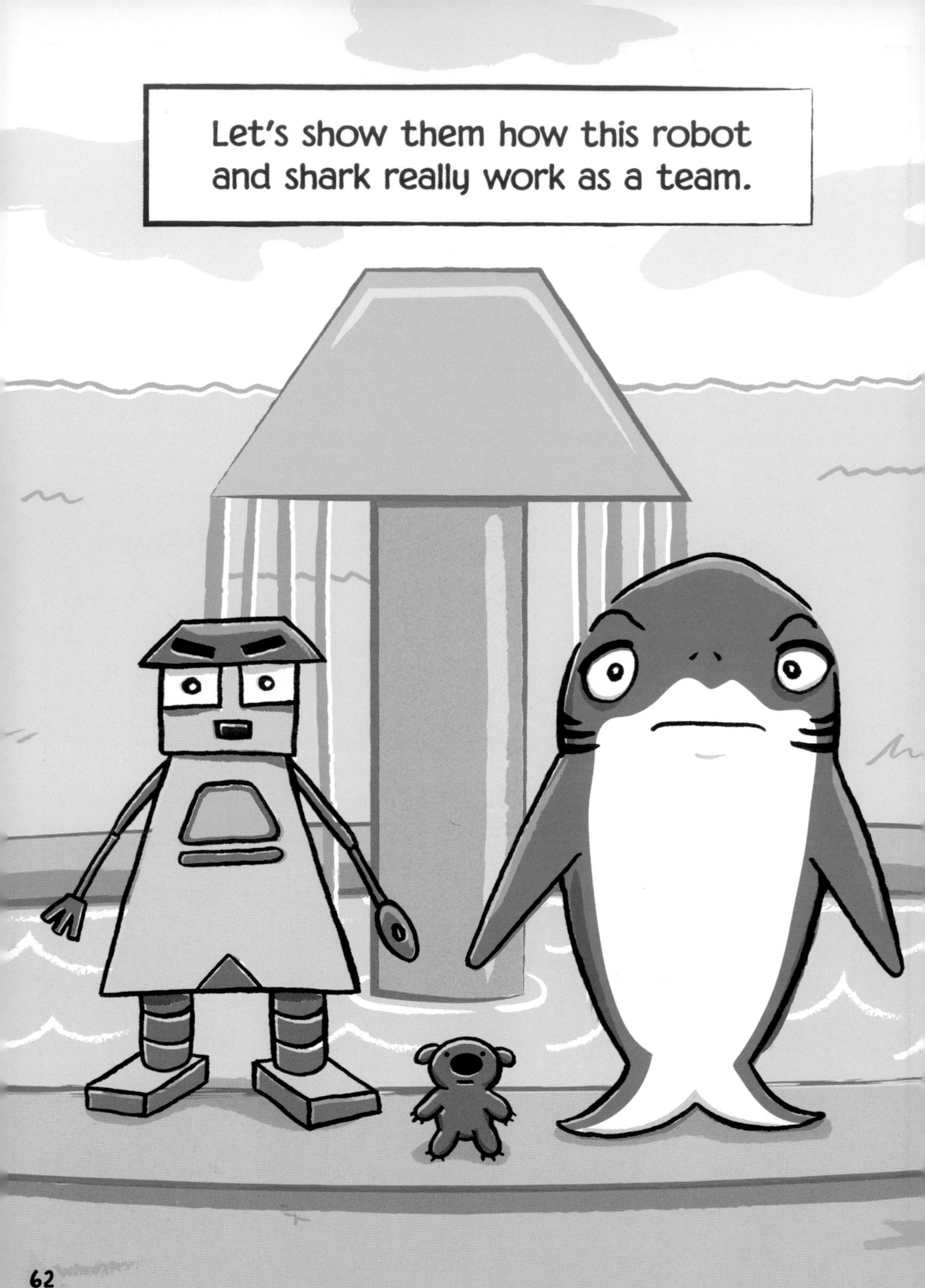
Let's show them how this robot and shark really work as a team.

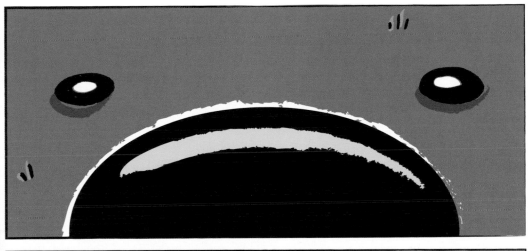

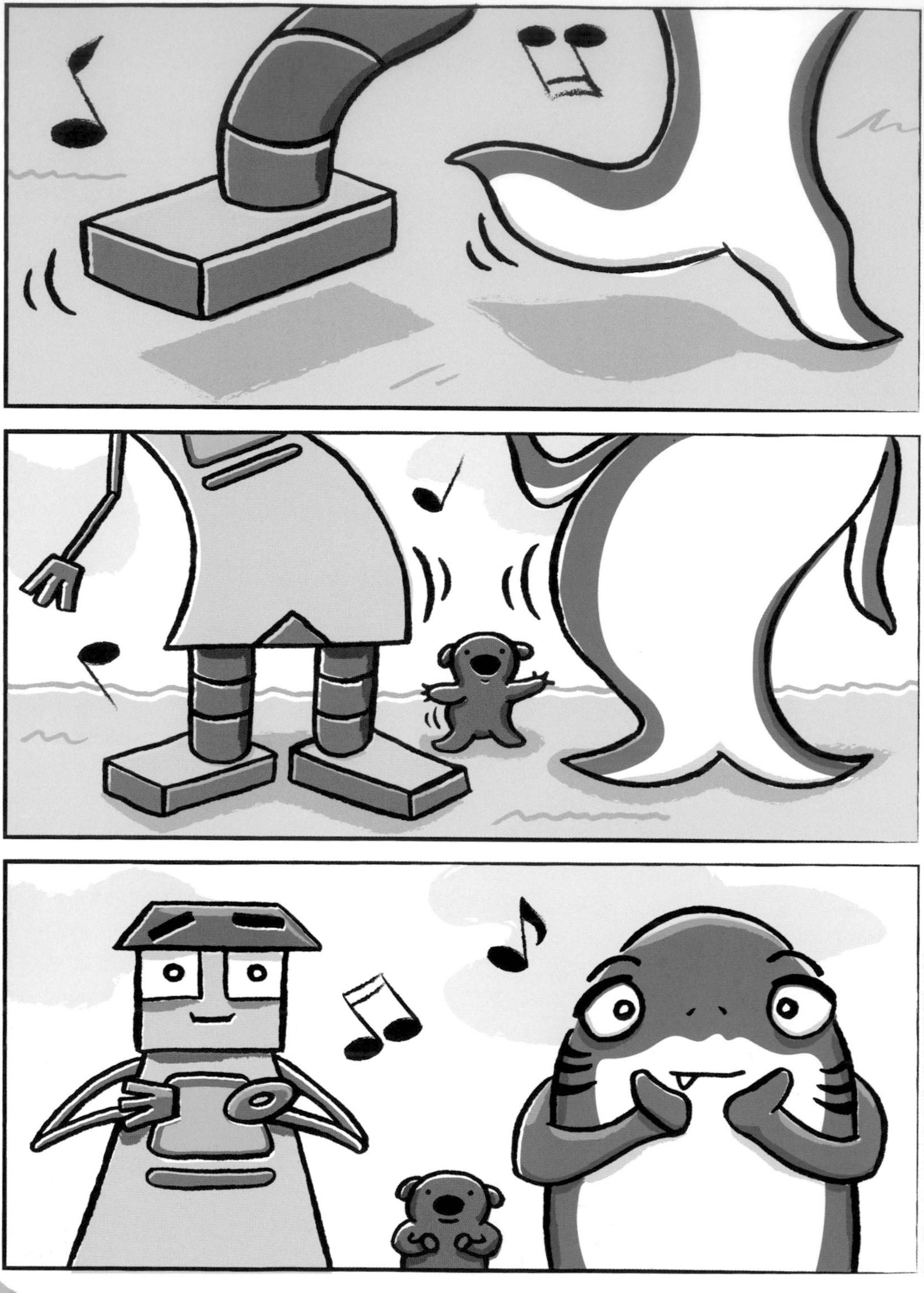

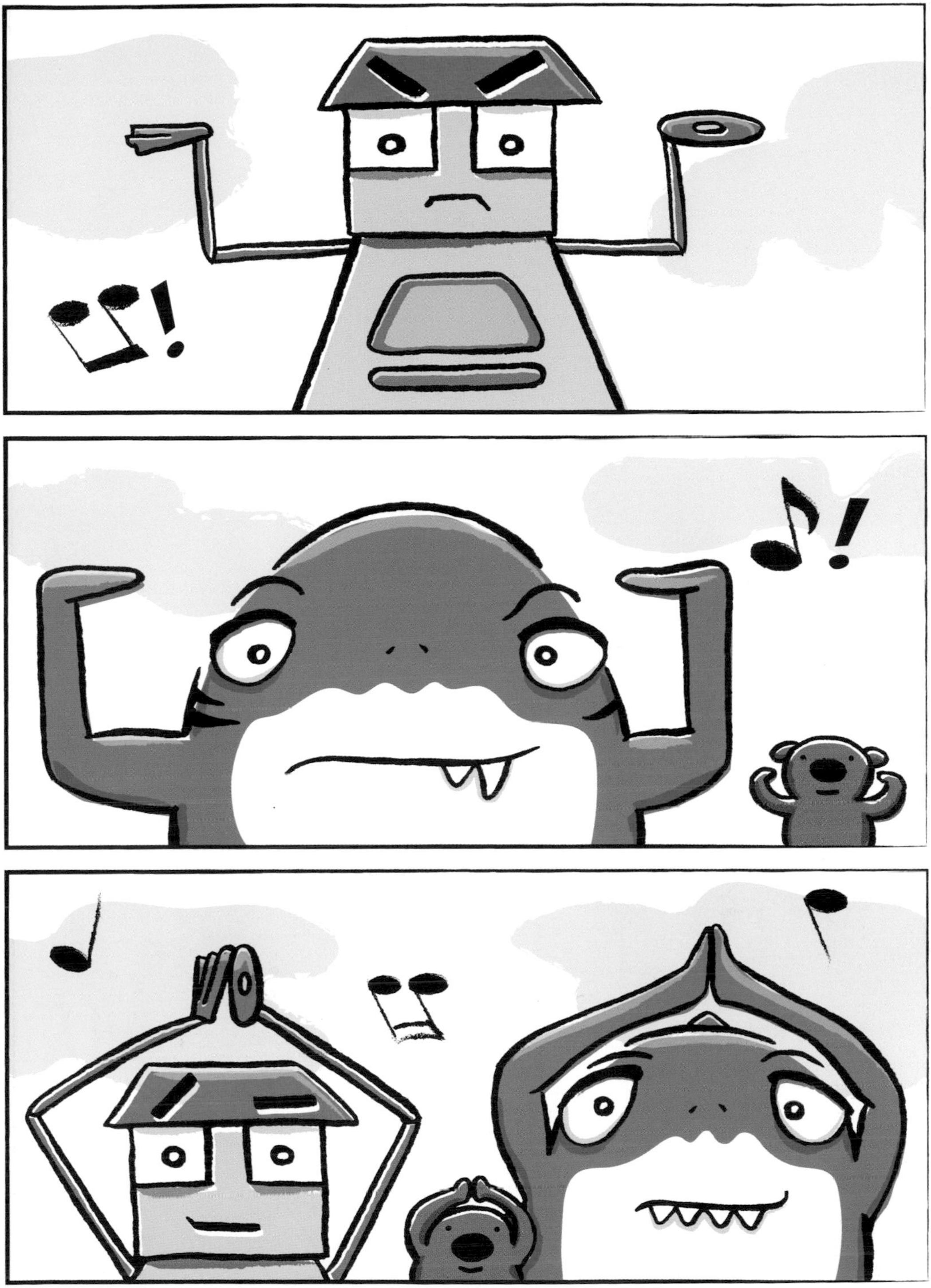

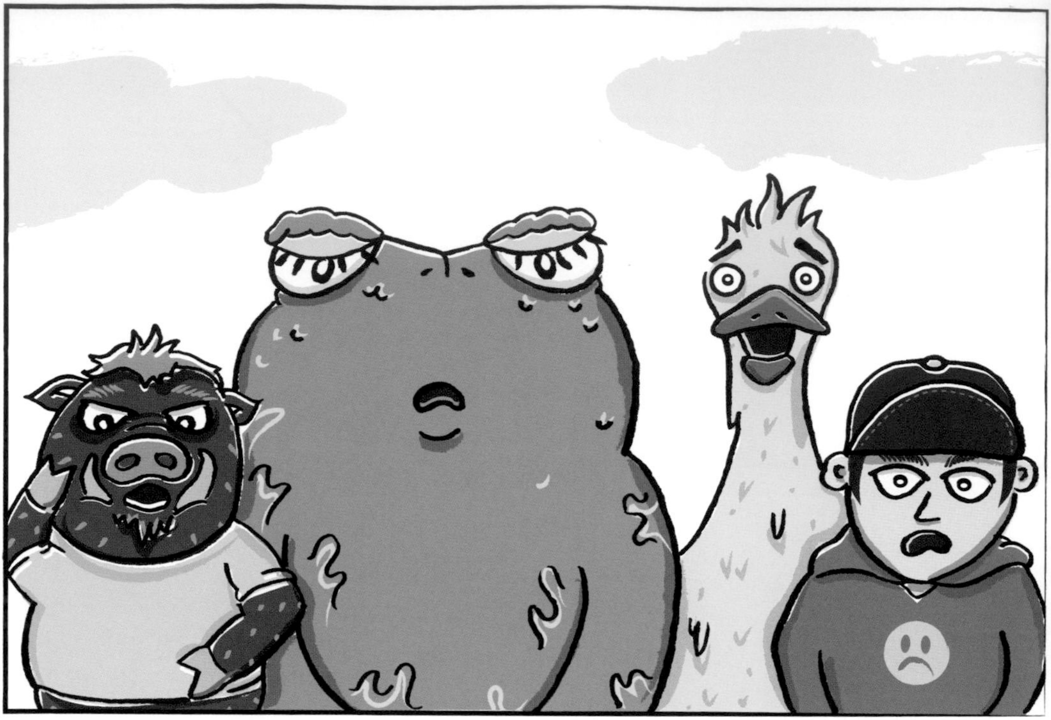

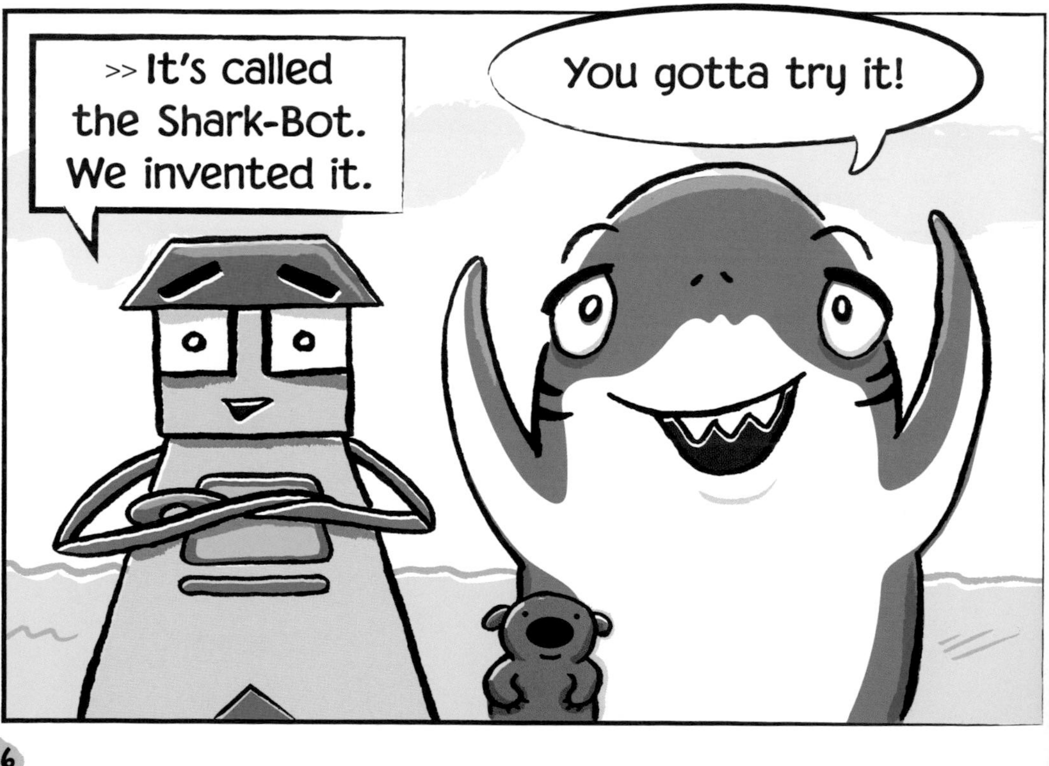
>> It's called the Shark-Bot. We invented it.
You gotta try it!

HOW TO DO THE SHARK-BOT

by SHARK and BOT

(1) STOMP **RIGHT** LIKE A ROBOT.

(2) STOMP LEFT LIKE A ROBOT.

* *

(3) WIGGLE YOUR SHOULDERS AND HIPS LIKE A SHARK.

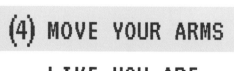

(4) MOVE YOUR ARMS LIKE YOU ARE SWIMMING THROUGH THE OCEAN.

* *

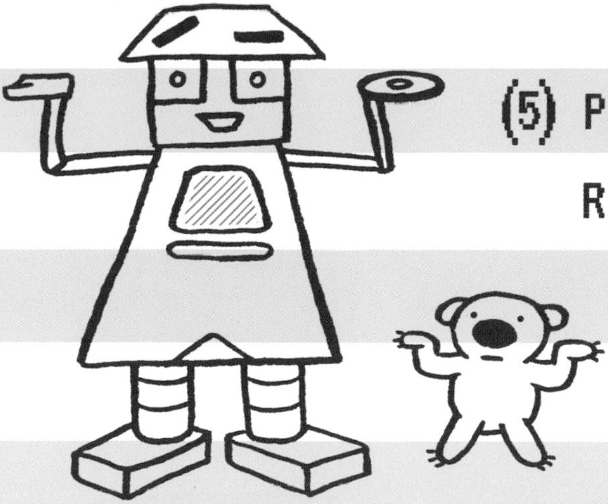

(5) PUT YOUR ROBOT HANDS OUT.

(6) PUT YOUR ROBOT HANDS IN.

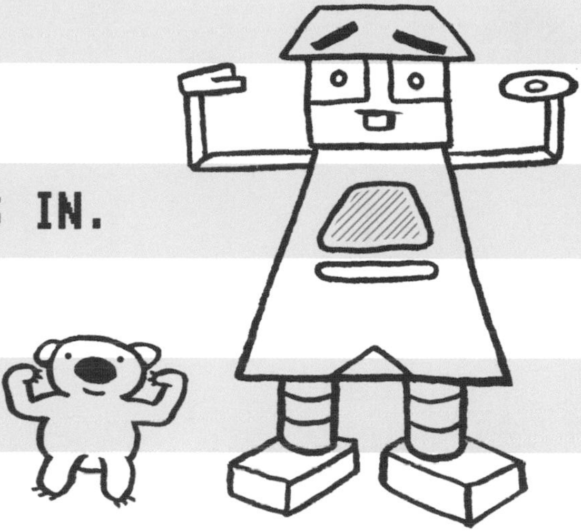

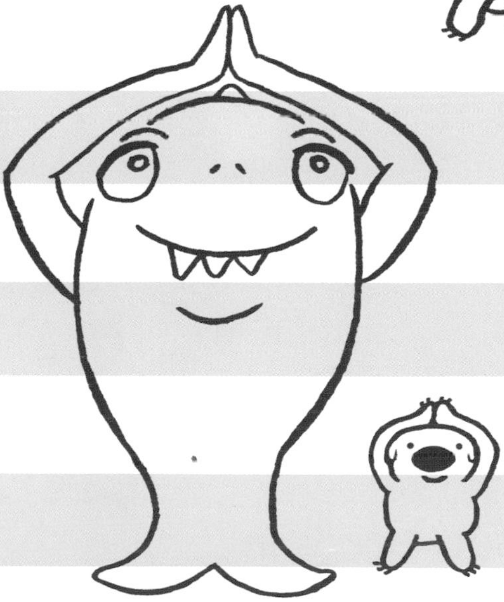

(7) RAISE YOUR HANDS UP TO MAKE A FIN.

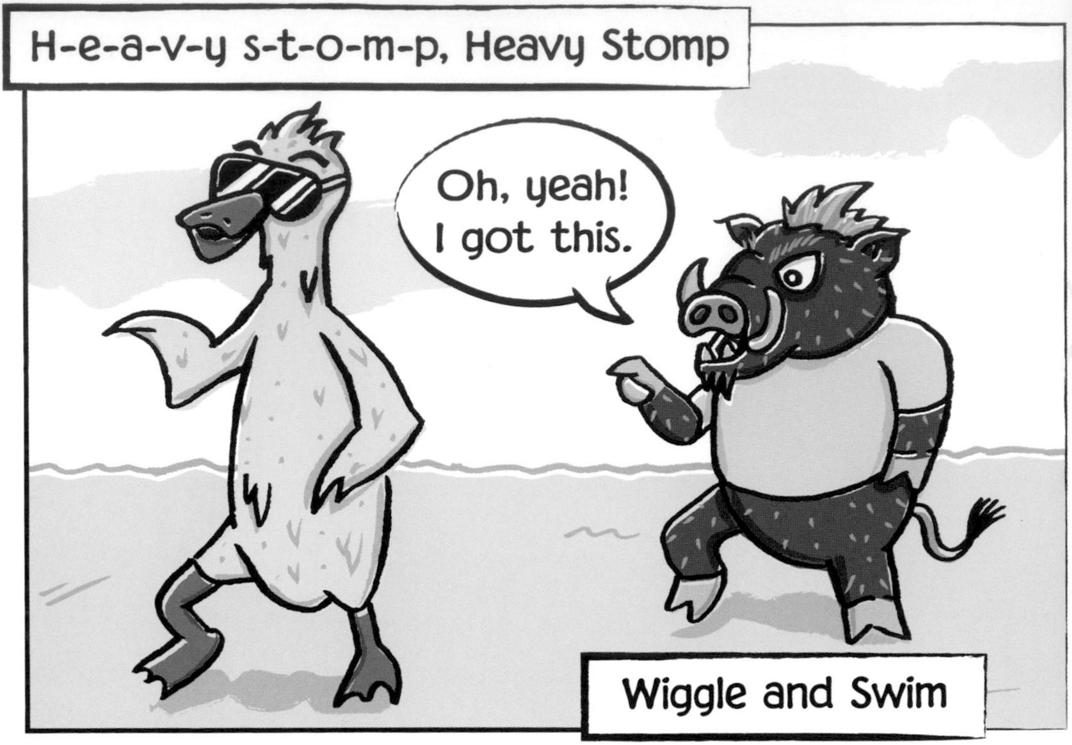
H-e-a-v-y s-t-o-m-p, Heavy Stomp
Oh, yeah! I got this.
Wiggle and Swim

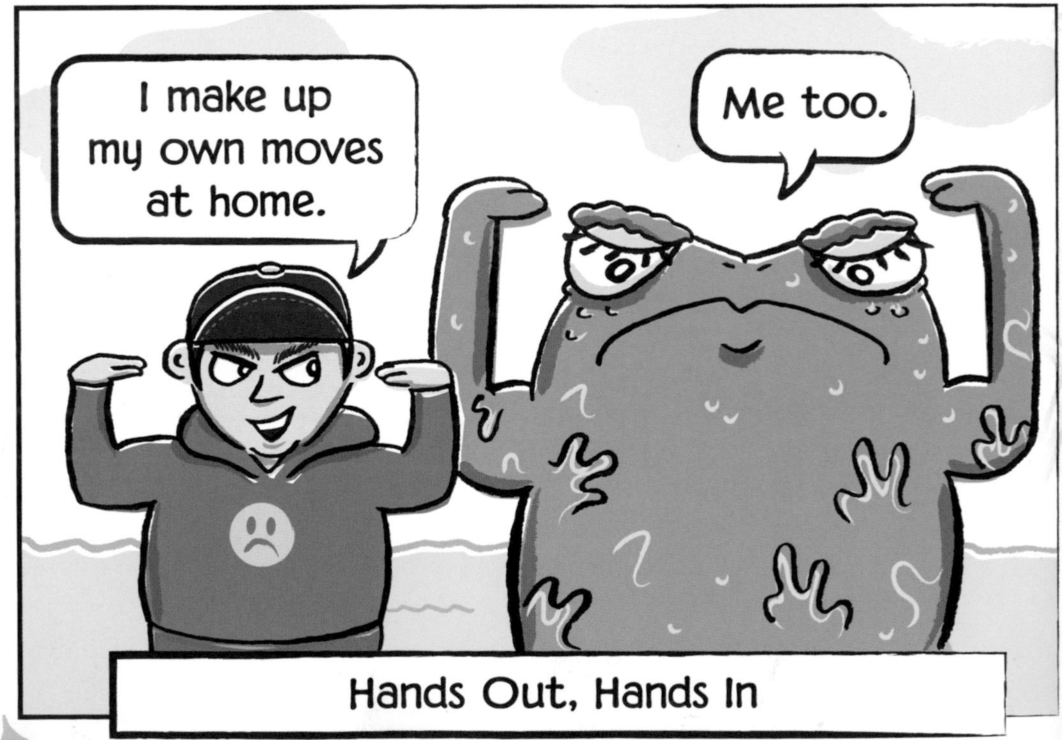
I make up my own moves at home.
Me too.
Hands Out, Hands In

Raise Your Fin

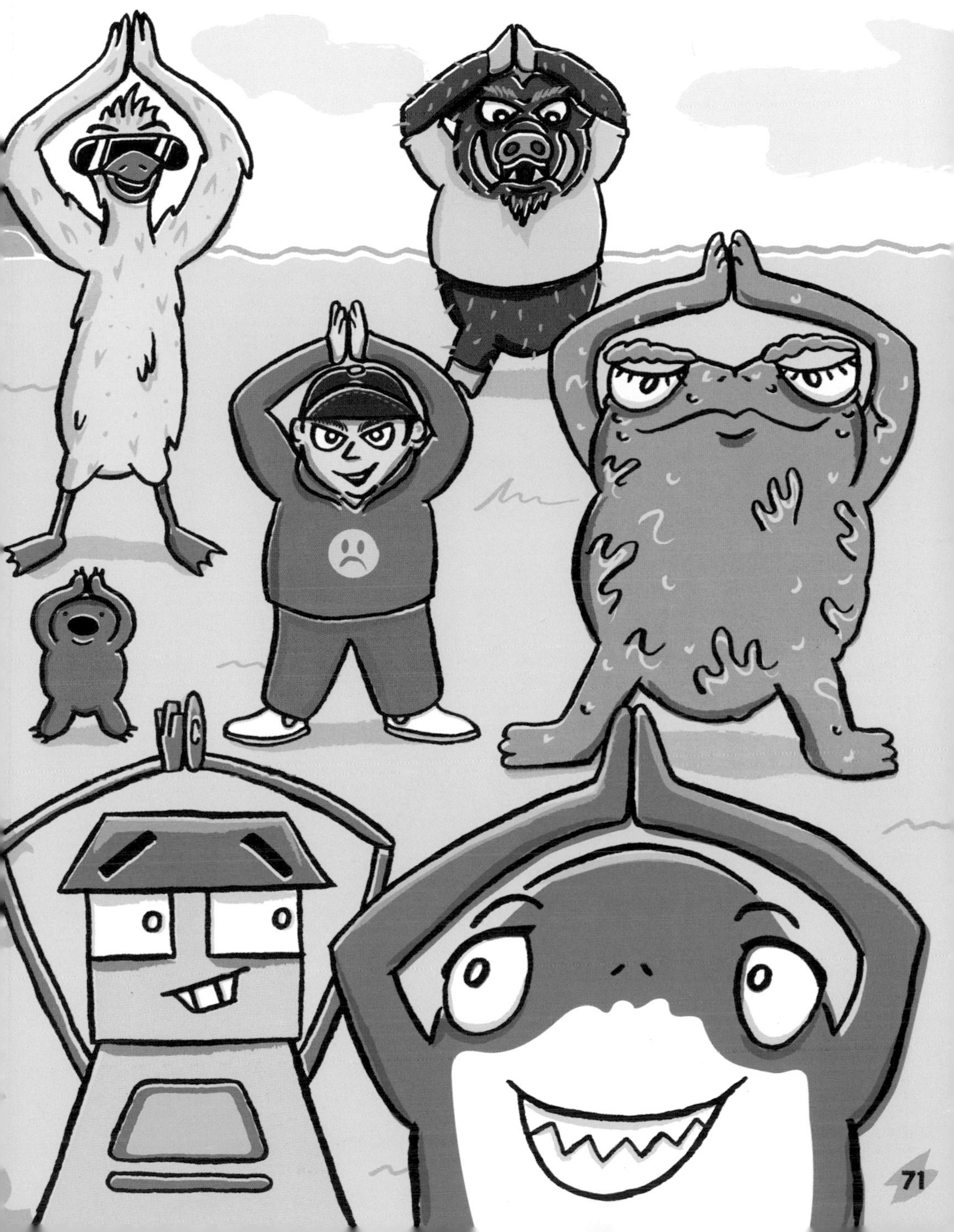

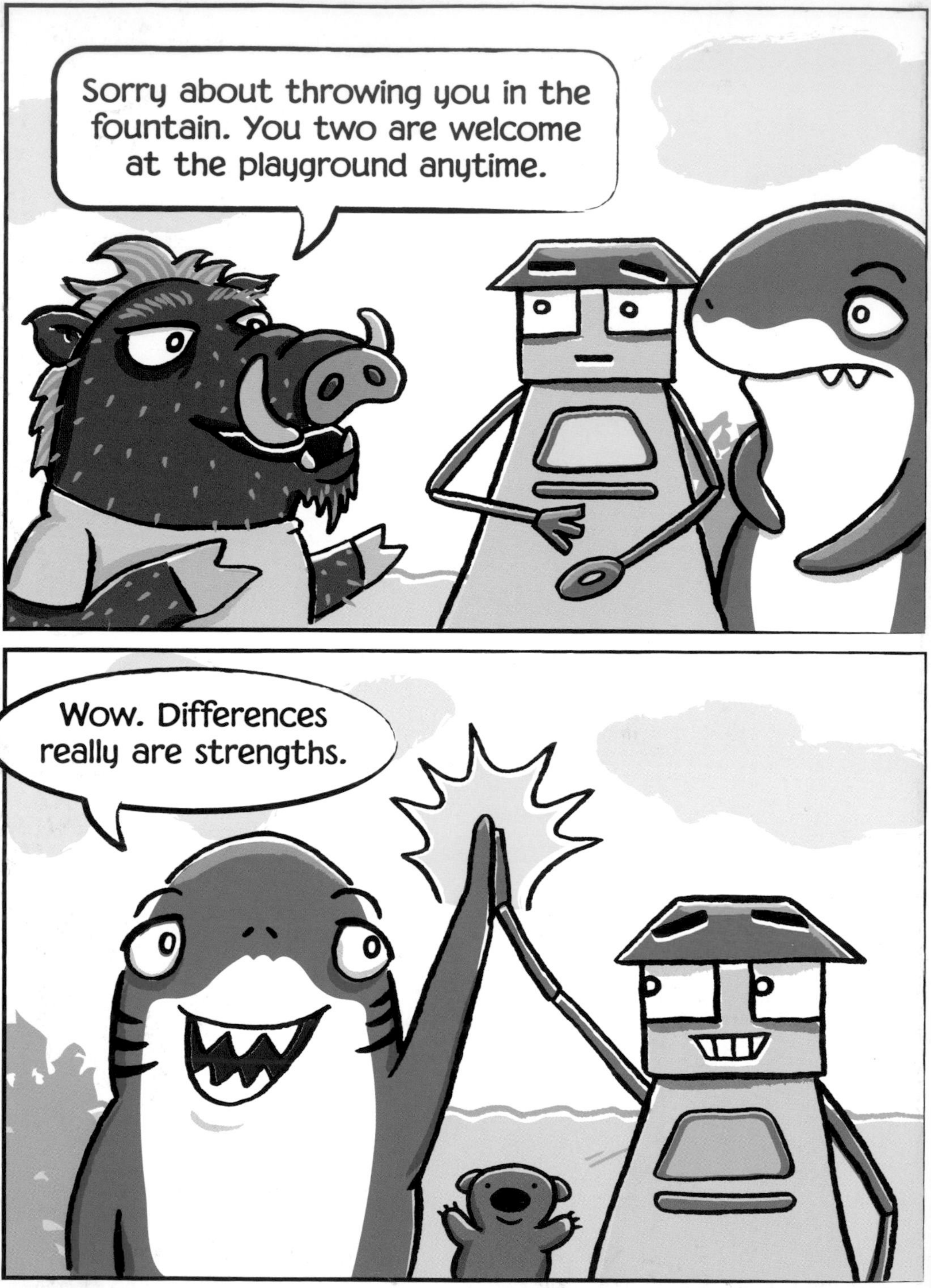
Sorry about throwing you in the fountain. You two are welcome at the playground anytime.
Wow. Differences really are strengths.

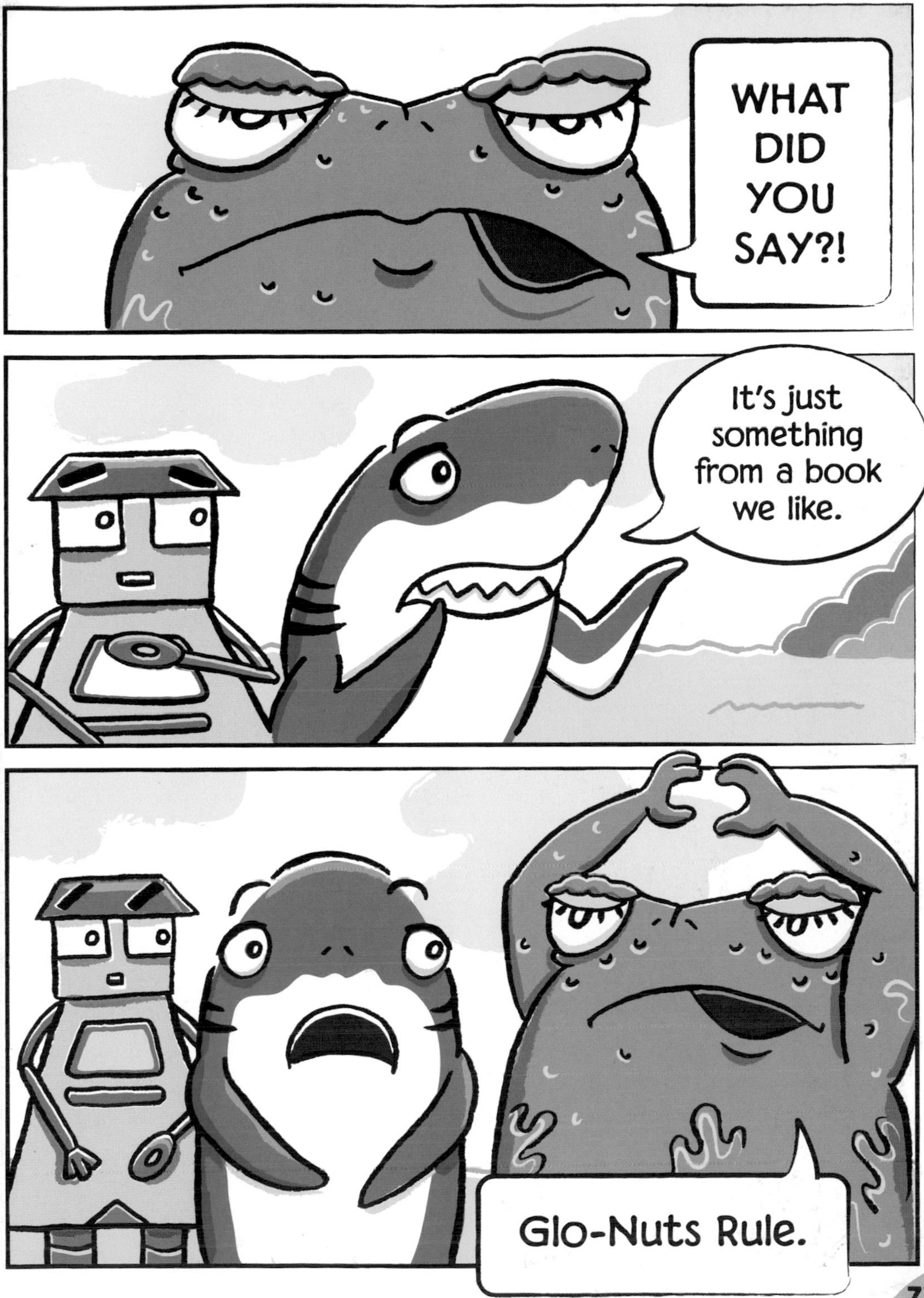
WHAT DID YOU SAY?!
It's just something from a book we like.
Glo-Nuts Rule.

Chapter 6

Friend-Ship Ahoy

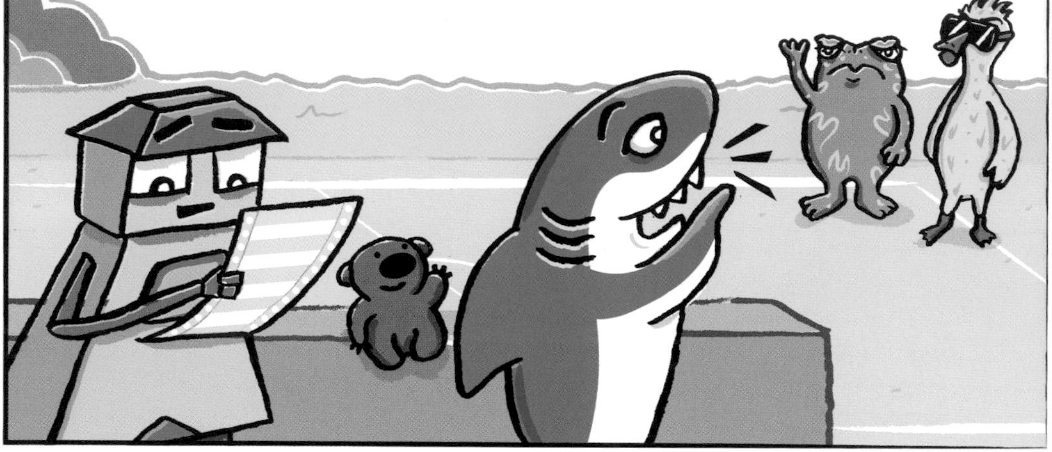

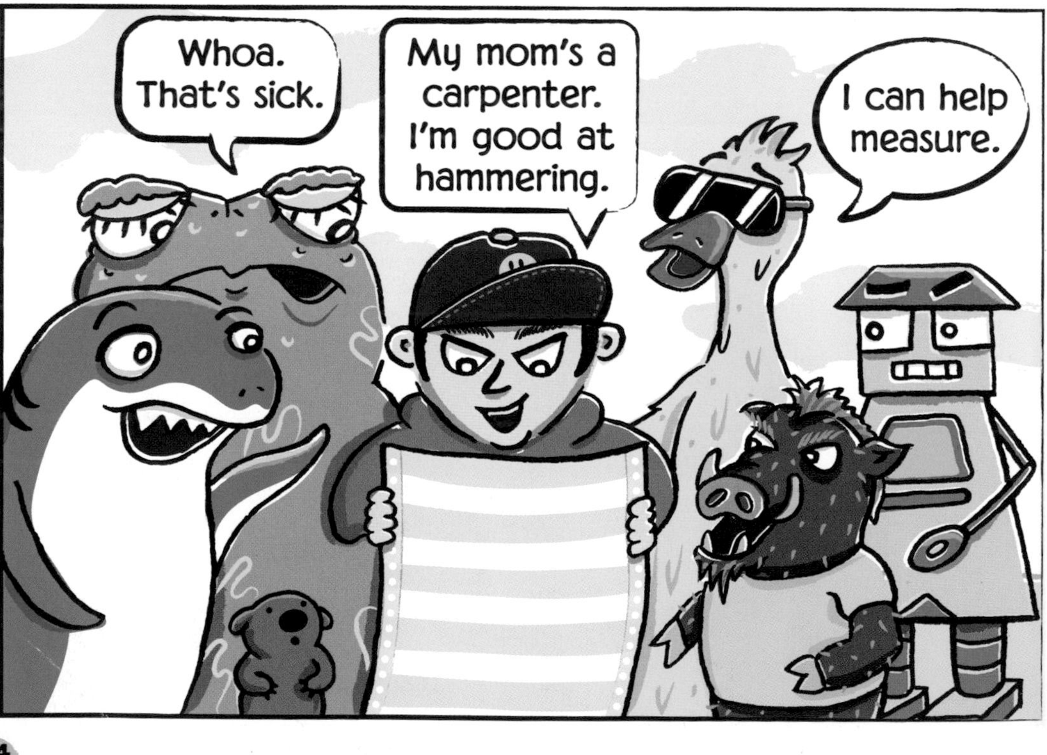
Whoa. That's sick.
My mom's a carpenter. I'm good at hammering.
I can help measure.

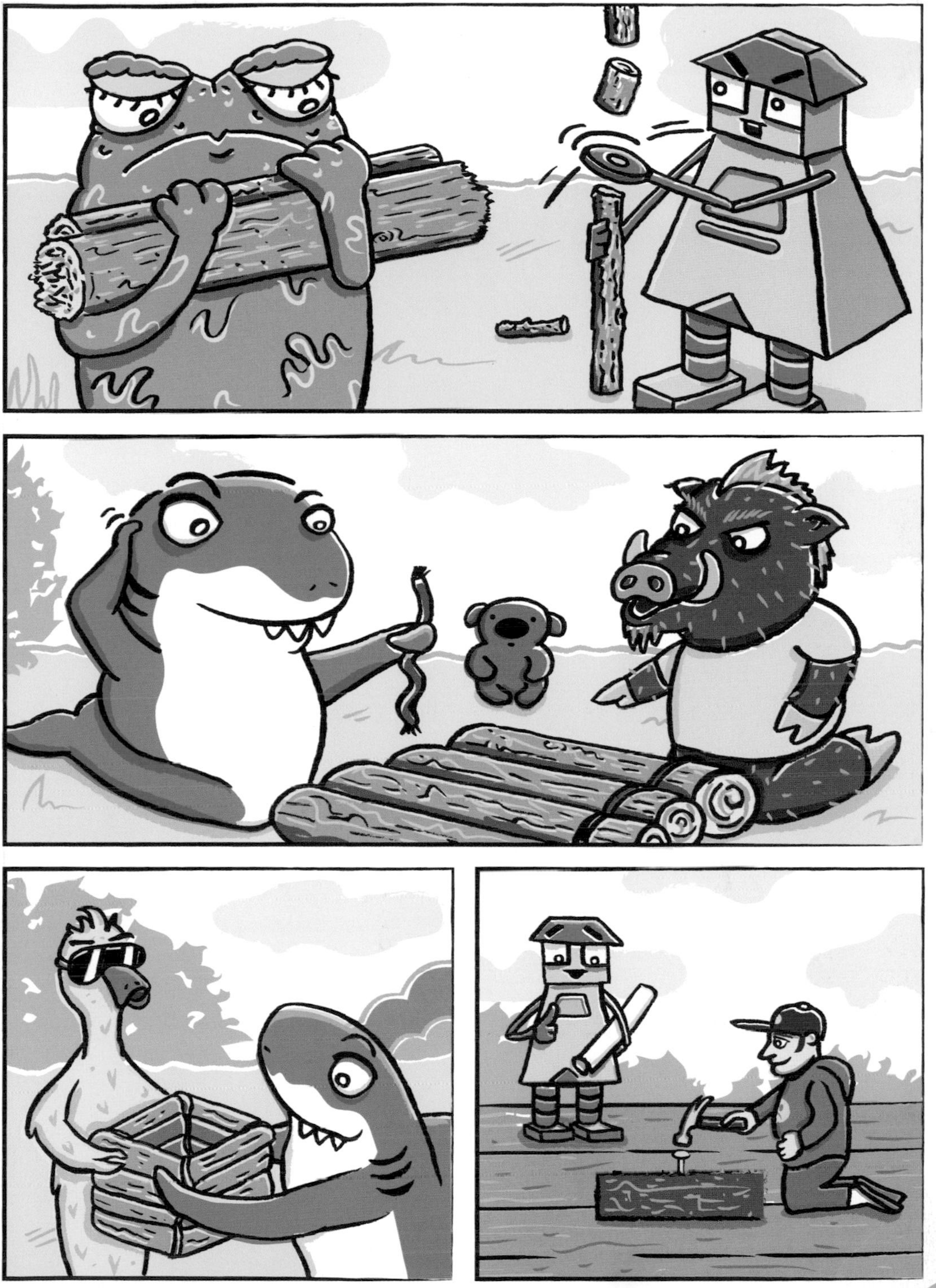

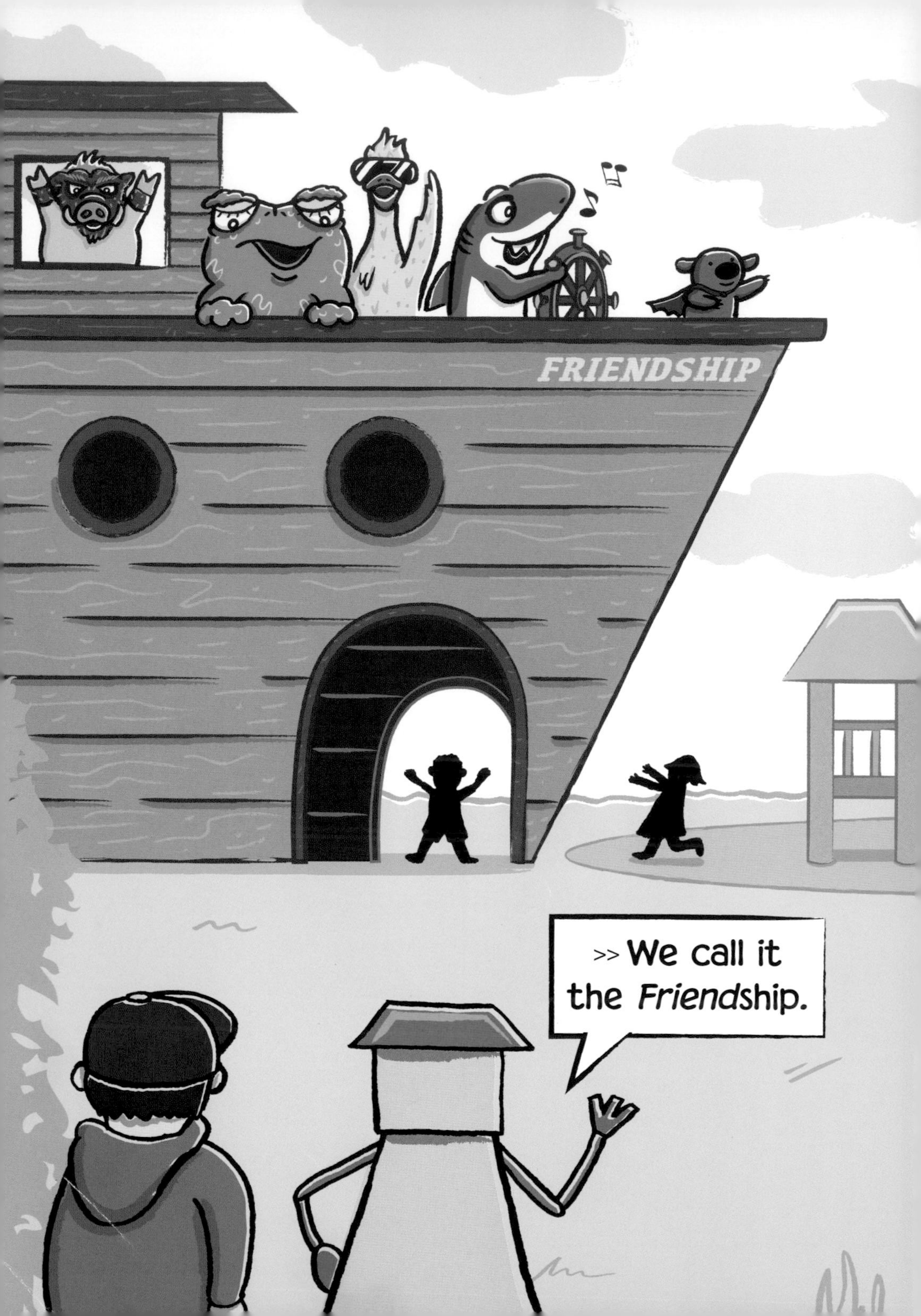
FRIENDSHIP
>> We call it the *Friendship.*

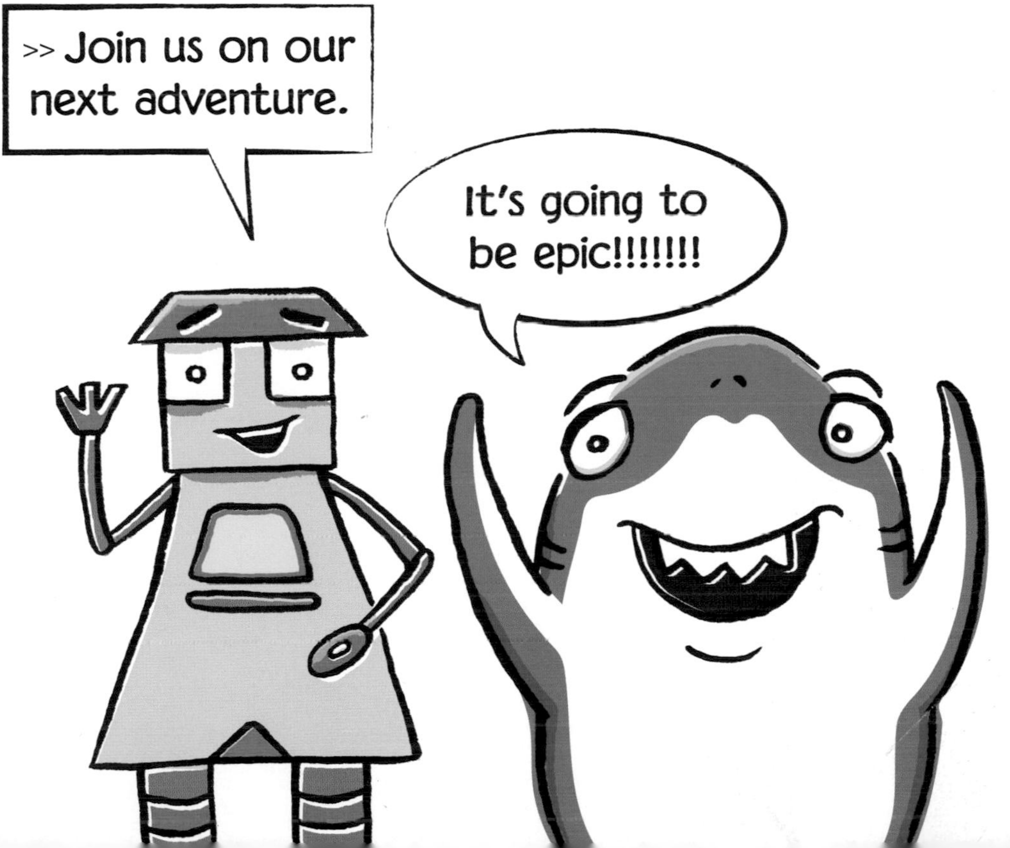
>> Join us on our next adventure.
It's going to be epic!!!!!!!!

BOT

MODEL: R-2300 Cutting Robot ("Cutter")

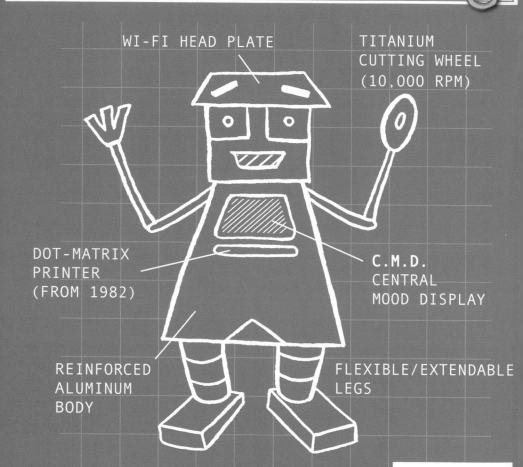

WI-FI HEAD PLATE

TITANIUM
CUTTING WHEEL
(10,000 RPM)

DOT-MATRIX
PRINTER
(FROM 1982)

C.M.D.
CENTRAL
MOOD DISPLAY

REINFORCED
ALUMINUM
BODY

FLEXIBLE/EXTENDABLE
LEGS

CAUTION:
DO NOT GET
NEAR WATER
OR LIQUIDS

BEHAVIOR:
• LOGICAL • MOODY
• A LITTLE BIT AWKWARD
• LOVES PLANNING
• EXCELLENT AT BUILDING

SHARK

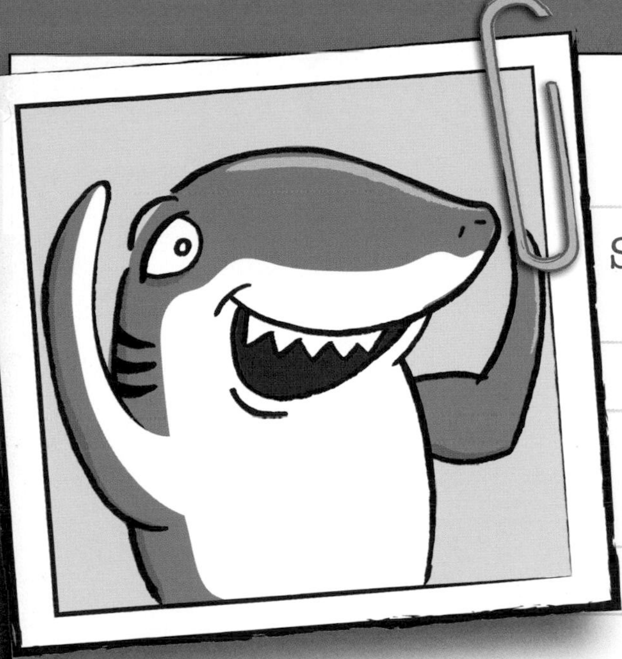

SPECIES:

GREAT WHITE

SCIENTIFIC NAME:

CARCHARODON CARCHARIAS

BEHAVIOR:

1. WHY IS THIS SHARK NEVER IN WATER?!!
2. VERY LOUD AND EXUBERANT, LOYAL
3. TERRIFIED OF SMALL THINGS (BUGS, MICE, POSSIBLY SNOWFLAKES)

KNOWN PARTNERS:

SPECIES: ~~RABBIT?~~ ~~MOUSE?~~ **WOMBAT**

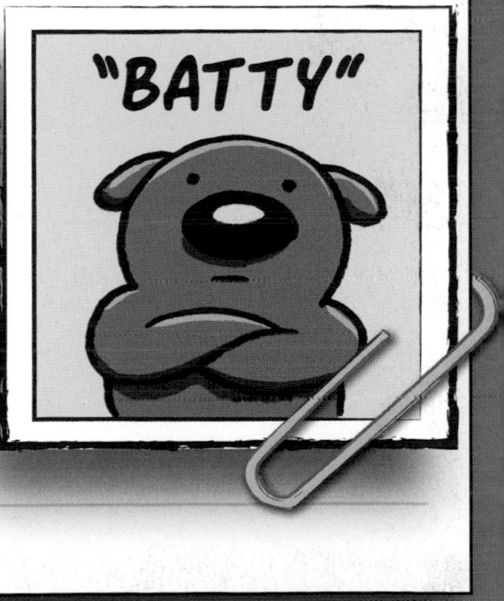
"BATTY"

SCIENTIFIC NAME:

VOMBATUS URSINUS

BEHAVIOR: ??

QUIET, POSSIBLE GENIUS

APPROACH WITH CAUTION

HOW TO DRAW SHARK

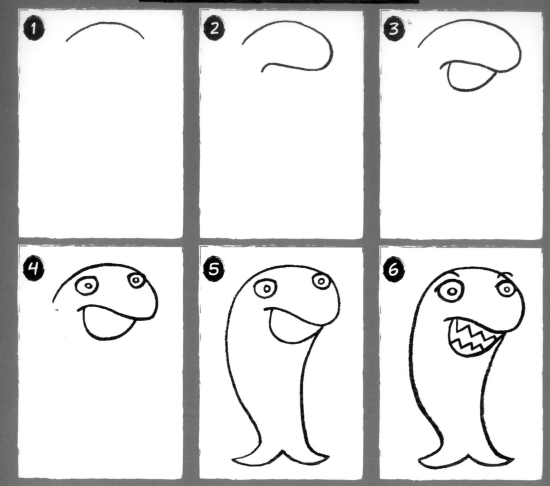

HOW TO DRAW BOT

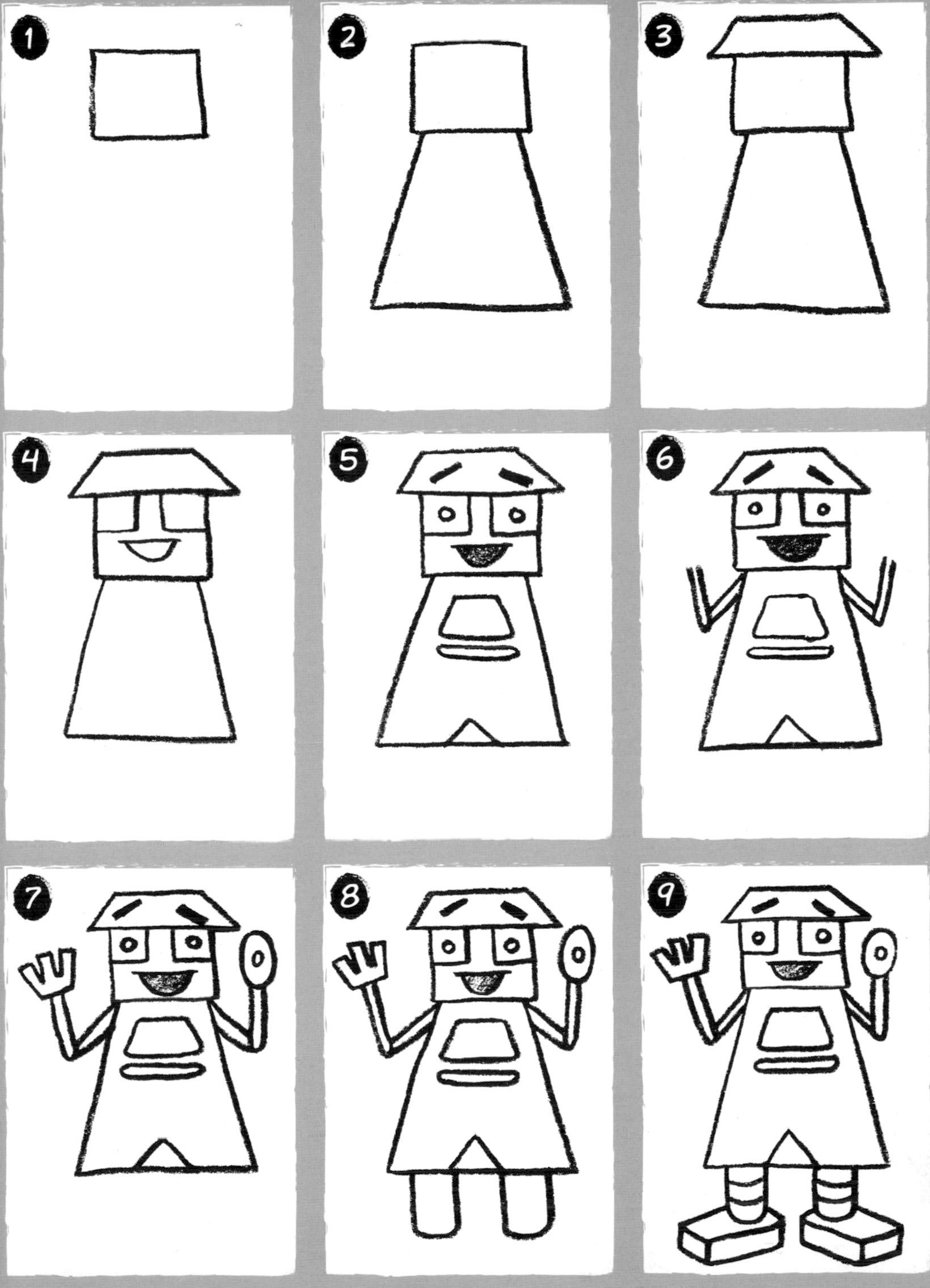
1
2
3
4
5
6
7
8
9

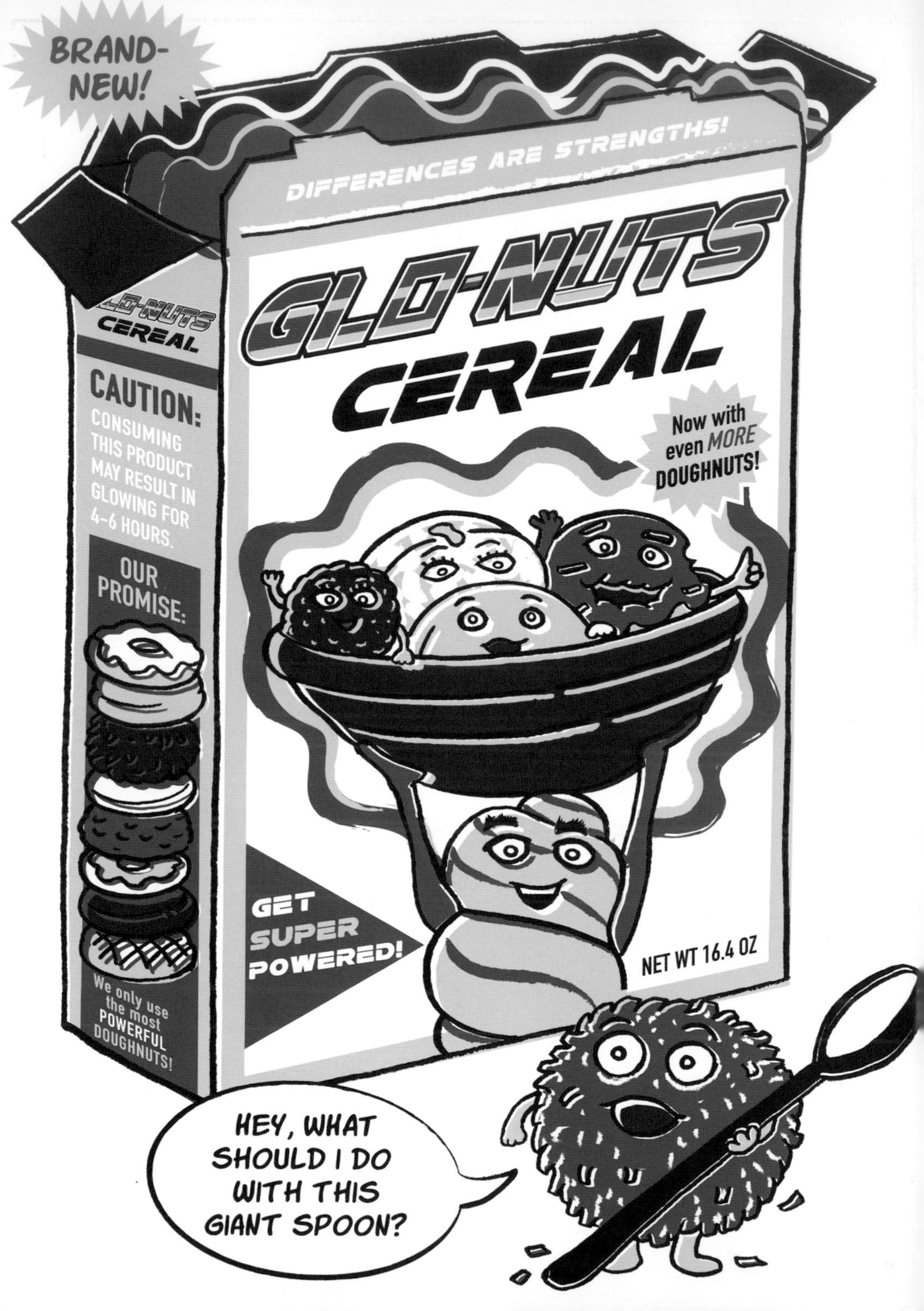
BRAND-NEW!
DIFFERENCES ARE STRENGTHS!
GLO-NUTS CEREAL
GLO-NUTS CEREAL
Now with even MORE DOUGHNUTS!
CAUTION: CONSUMING THIS PRODUCT MAY RESULT IN GLOWING FOR 4-6 HOURS.
OUR PROMISE:
We only use the most POWERFUL DOUGHNUTS!
GET SUPER POWERED!
NET WT 16.4 OZ
HEY, WHAT SHOULD I DO WITH THIS GIANT SPOON?

Brian Yanish has worked for Jim Henson Productions, trained as a special effects mold maker, written and performed comedy, and designed educational software, apparel, furniture, and toys. He is the creator of ScrapKins®, a recycled arts program that inspires kids to see creative potential in everyday junk. Brian has presented workshops at schools around the world and even appeared on *Sesame Street*. He lives in Rochester, New York, and enjoys sharks, robots, and gummy things.

brianyanish.com

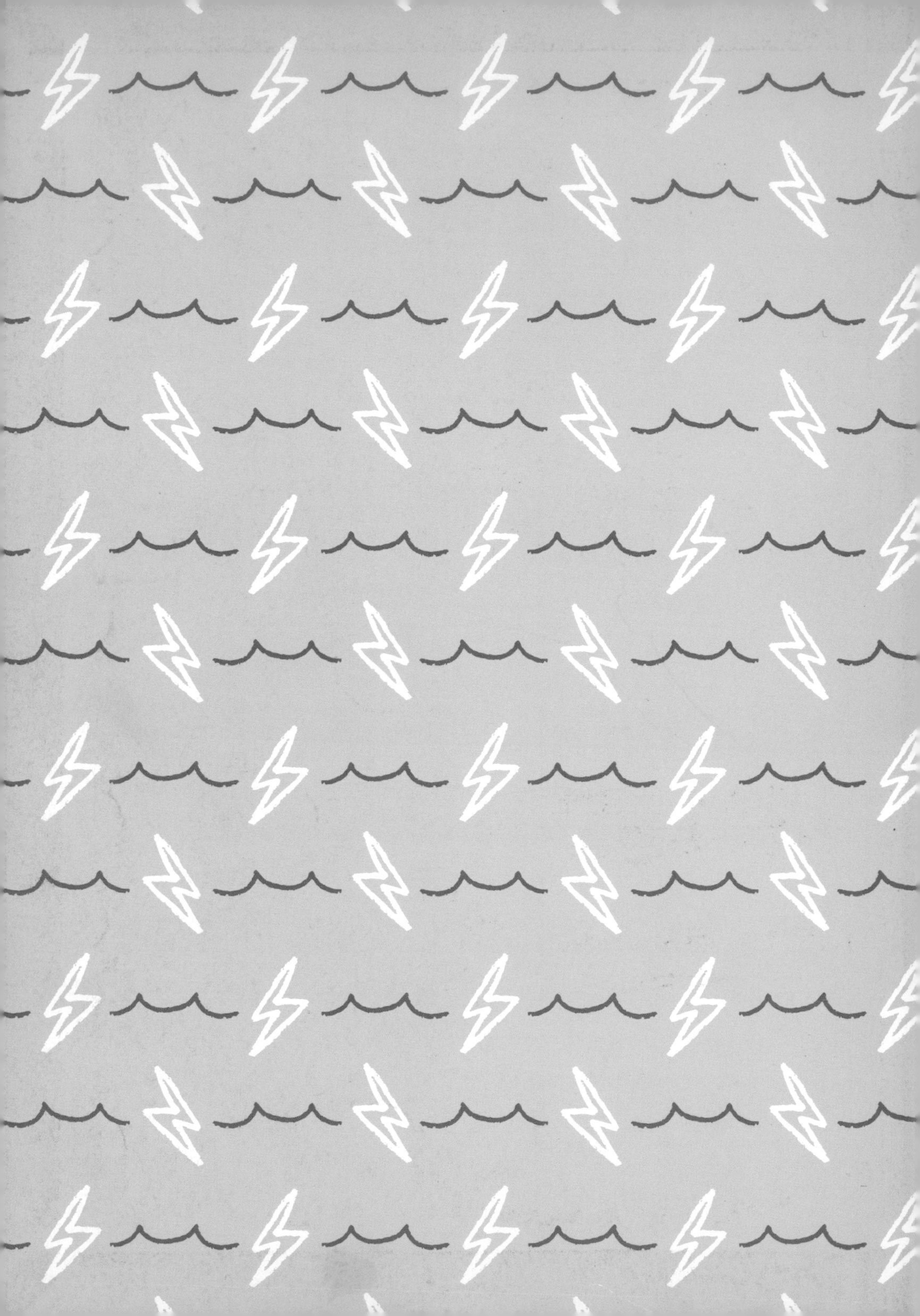